SHEMEKA MITCHELL

VINDICTIVE

BLACK HOUSE PUBLISHING
Killeen

VINDICTIVE

Black House Publishing Edition, April 2014
Published in the United States by Black House Publishing, Texas.

ISBN-13: 978-0-9911528-0-3

Editing: Shontrell Wade
Interior Design: A Reader's Perspective
Cover Photography: Taria Reed - www.TariaReed.net
Cover Models:Kenny Williams, Tanisha Frazier and Angelina Cavanaugh

www.bhousepublishing.com

Printed in the United States of America

10 9 8 7 6 5 4 3 2 1

ALSO AVAILABLE FROM SHEMEKA MITCHELL

Rendezvous In Vegas
Everlasting Love - Book 1
Tainted Lies - Book 2
Blind Trust - Book 3
Endless Love - Book 4
Misplaced Loyalty - Book 5

Coming Soon!

For The Love Of All Things Chocolate
Loving Leslie
Boy Toy
The Art Of Forgiveness

SHEMEKA MITCHELL
VINDICTIVE

CHAPTER ONE

WHERE, OH where, did my motivation go? If anyone has seen her, please let the bitch know that I'm looking for her ass and I need her to return to me immediately.

Kat sat watching Supernatural and surfing the internet, despite having a ton of housework that needed to be done. Plus, it was the end of a big merger at her job. She had to prepare two exams for the new hires and had to be up early for work. She just couldn't seem to get into her groove. She was thinking about it, but doing nothing. Instead, her mind was in the clouds. Daydreaming about him again, imagining them being together, taking their friendship to the next level. If only she hadn't found the courage to let him know how she felt.

"Would you like to go to dinner?" she asked.

"Are you kidding me? Are you fucking serious? Do I look like I'm interested in dating you? You are out of your fucking mind, and I would appreciate it if you stayed the hell away from me."

Kat stood with a stunned look on her face. "Why are you saying this?"

"Because I don't have time for simple-minded bitches coming up in my face looking for a fuck. I'm not interested. Get a hobby, join a fucking gym, or some shit. Just get the fuck out of my face," he barked.

And with that, he walked out of the break room to the laughter of their fellow coworkers.

Kat made her way to her car and cried her eyes out. She left work early that day and took the next one off. She was beyond humiliated and heartbroken by the fact that she had laid everything on the line by approaching him.

His rejection hurt like hell and she felt like a complete fool. Now, she was walking around at work full of shame and with her head down. Even after all of that, she was still attracted to him. And not just the normal, run-of-the-mill, little attraction. Her shit was full-blown lust. She was thinking of that man every night—wet dreams with him in the starring role.

Kat sighed, deciding to call it a night and rest up for work. She needed to get a grip soon, before she ended up doing some shit that she would regret in the future.

Once she entered the land of slumber, images invaded her mind…

I walk him to the door. "Thanks for keeping me company tonight."

"No problem. I had fun. We should do it more often." He turns toward me and pulls me into his arms for a hug. The warmth of his embrace seeps in to my soul. I feel safe. He doesn't release me. Instead, he tightens his hold, so I do the same. I'm following his lead, hoping we are on the path to so much more. Slowly, he loosens his grip, but doesn't completely let me go. He looks into my eyes for a moment before speaking again. "You are so beautiful."

I was not expecting him to say that. My mouth drops open, but I catch myself. "Umm, thanks."

He doesn't say anything, just continues to look at me. I begin to feel a little uncomfortable. He seems to notice it, because he then leans in and let his lips connect with mine. My heart is pounding, my ears are ringing. His lips are covering mine in a most succulent kiss.

It has been so long since I've been kissed. Wow. Is this what I have been missing? I hope he doesn't think that he is just going to kiss me and leave. Oh no, he's awakened a desire, started a fire that is beginning to consume me. And I need him to extinguish the flames.

"I knew you would taste so sweet." His eyelids are low. "I want more," he tells me as he claims what he wants.

I have no desire to stop him. In fact, I pull him closer to me and wrap my arms around his neck. More, I want more. I need more. Finally, he pulls back and we look at one another.

"I want you to fuck me." I cannot believe that I said that. Maybe my courage comes from the drinks I consumed earlier.

"Are you sure that is what you want?" His look is telling me that he wants the same thing.

"Yes, I am very sure."

"Okay."

That is all he said as I lead him to my room. I haven't been with a man in over three years. My need intensifies as we caress one another. His touch is gentle, but mine is greedy. He lets me take whatever I want. He allows me to be in control.

I want to taste him from head to toe. His body is so very beautiful. My kisses start from his head and continue down. His swollen member becomes the object of my attention. I kiss and lick it until he can't stand it any longer. I rise up and rub my breast over his dick. He gasps as I place small kisses over his abs. I am having so much fun. He tastes delightful. After a while, I guess he's had enough, because he flips me onto my back and climbs on top of me.

"My turn," he says with hunger in his eyes.

Oh yes, I am ready for this. At least I think I am. "What are you planning on doing to me?" I ask.

"Hmmm… Whatever I want." He looks at me as if he's daring me to deny him his treasure.

"Is that right?"

"Yes. I promise it will be good for you." He answers full of confidence. I hope I haven't bitten off more than I can chew. Whatever. I am a grown ass woman, and right now, it's on.

"Give it to me." I demand, ready for whatever he has in mind.

His eyes hold fire as he looks at my mouth. And he does exactly what I asked. He takes my body on an incredible ride. He makes me feel things that I have never experienced. His dick touches spots deep within. His kisses hold so much passion. My mind is reeling with such pleasure.

"Eric," I cry out as he brings me to yet another orgasm.

"Yes, baby?" He doesn't stop stroking me and I can't stop exploding.

"Oh, baby. Oh yes. Please?"

"Please what, love?" he taunts me.

"I don't know."

"Please stop?" He is enjoying this.

"Please don't stop, please give it to me, and please whatever."

He laughs at my answers. The way he is going, he has no intention of stopping anytime soon. Damn, this man is doing my body justice.

"Fuck. This ... this is mine now. You know that, right?" He says it like I might resist.

Oh no, buddy, never that. He can have whatever the heck he wants. Literally.

"If you want it."

"Oh, I want it. All of it." He is claiming me as his, all the while still stroking me.

Shit, how many times does he plans on making me nut? My mind is blank. I can no longer focus on anything other than him. The pressure is so intense that I think I may pass out, but he doesn't stop. Instead, he goes deeper and faster. He places his lips around my nipple and sucks hard. I am no longer aware of my surroundings. My body is betraying me, as if it is in cahoots with him. I know he knows this, because I hear him chuckle lightly. He's amused at the amount of pleasure he's giving me. He is delighted that he can play me so well.

"So delicious, baby," he whispers in my ear. I feel his tongue trace the outline of it.

CHAPTER 2

"FUUUUUUCCKKK," KAT said to her empty room. "That was the best dream ever and this God-forsaken alarm clock just had to go off."

Damn, she at least wanted to cum one more time. Shit. She still felt a nice sensation between her legs. She reached down to check her panties; they were soaked. That damn man had the ability to make her cum over and over in her dreams. Now, she had to get ready to face him at work while thinking about all of the naughty things he had done to her body in that delightful dream. Well, what-the-fuck-ever. It was time to get up and make that money.

Uuuuggh, Kat did not like mornings. She wished she could just stay in bed until noon every damn day, but, oh no, she had to be in the office at eight on the dot. In order for that to happen, she needed to get up around six so that she could drag around and overdose on coffee then shower. She wished that she could be a morning person, but that shit just wasn't happening for her.

She lay in bed with her eyes closed, trying to convince herself that it was okay to get in another thirty minutes of sleep, but also thinking that if she did, she was going to oversleep and be late for work. Being late for work was definitely not an option. Especially not with the Queen Bitch as her boss.

The Queen Bitch ran a tight ship and played no games. In her book, no excuse was acceptable for being late. Well, unless the employee was dead, but then she was so ruthless that she just might revive that person just to fire their ass for dying in the first place.

Kat knew that she should not be listening to office gossip surrounding her boss, especially since it was another sister doing the damn thang in the workplace. She was definitely someone young girls could look up to. Employees made jokes about how she ran the office, but they all had respect for the way she got things done. And she was not a plain Jane either. She had a body to make any woman envious, skin the color of caramel, hazel eyes. Her own long, thick, dark brown hair hung down her back. Kat did not really know her heritage, but she knew that her ass was mixed with something. She was betting on Mexican and Black.

The woman was absolutely beautiful. Most of the men at the office wanted to be with her. Most of the women wanted to look like her. It had to be hard for her, knowing that she was wanted by all. Bitch. Kat often wondered how it would feel to have men ogling after her in that way. She guessed that they were just not interested in a well-endowed sista. She could see that green-eyed demon rearing its ugly head. Time to think about something else. She really did not want to be known as that jealous-type bitch. She was determined not to let her negative thoughts about her own body damage her confidence. She was tired of comparing her body to other women. Every time she did that, she ended up feeling depressed. Her focus was on the future and securing it for herself and, hopefully, her future children. And that meant taking her behind to work each and every single day.

Hell, even find a mate one day, she thought as she started the shower. She had been single for so long because she was absolutely tired of dealing with men and their drama. They always claim that women have all the drama, but in Kat's life, they were usually the ones with the baggage. She tried to stay drama-free and stress-free and have a happy existence. She was not gonna lie and say that she did not have any baggage—she did—but she thought she carried it well. Maybe she was too damn independent. That could be the reason she was still single.

Kat didn't know, but she did know that she could not stand a weak-ass, whiny man. How could a man be her rock when his ass complained more than she did? She guessed that she would remain single for the rest of her days, since she had no intention of ever supporting a man who did not deserve it. She understood a woman having her man's back in emergencies. Her problem was when guys asked that of her before the relationship even had a chance to begin. It was the wrong way to start a relationship and expect it to last. Maybe she wasn't meant to have a man at all. She promised herself that she would never settle for less than she felt she deserved.

CHAPTER 3

AS SOON as Kat walked out of the elevator, she noticed Angela, the Queen Bitch, on the prowl. She had exactly two minutes to make it to her desk before she got her ass handed to her on a platter. Speed walking, she made it just in time.

"Damn, I thought I was going to have the privilege of actually firing your ass today," Angela called across the office.

Kat looked over her shoulder. "No, not today. But who knows what may happen tomorrow."

Angela rolled her eyes. "Smart ass." She walked into her office and closed the door.

Christy, Kat's one and only friend at the office, shook her head. "Girl, you know she is just itching to fire your ass."

"I know, but ask me if I give a fuck."

"Do you give a fuck?" she asked.

"Hell, fuck no, I hate this freaking place," Kat said while arranging the folders on her desk. "It's not so much the job; it's the people that I don't really care for." She booted up her computer and logged in. "Most of the men are dogs and the women just let them get away with any and everything."

Christy looked over at Kat and asked, "Are you still upset about what happened with Eric?"

"Girl, no. I am so over Eric Lefevre" Kat lied quickly. Deep down, she knew she was still upset and a little hurt about what went down with him. "He is a male whore just like the rest of them. And you know what they want."

She had never admitted to Christy—or anyone for that matter—just how much that man's actions and words hurt her. That shit hurt down to the core of her soul, and she was trying hard as hell to work her way back from that without having resentment in her heart. It was a struggle, especially since she had to see him every damn day. So, unless he quit or one of them got fired, she guessed she had to find a way to deal. She really did not want to look for another job; she wasn't up for that shit. So, she was going to get past this if it was the last thing she did.

If only other people would let her forget her very public humiliation by Eric, though. Someone always brought it back up. A couple of Eric's friends often poked fun when they happened to be around one another at the same time. Mark would say, "Hey, Eric, there's your girlfriend," or some other stupid crap that made her retreat into her shell. A few times, she saw Eric give him a pointed look that made him shut up on the spot. Other times, he would just ignore him and keep on eating his lunch.

Whenever Eric attempted to speak to Kat, she would mumble "Hello," and continue on her way. She was determined to move on with her life and be happy, vowing to get rid of all the romantic feelings that she had for him.

Kat thought back to the day that she had approached him. She had finally convinced herself that it was time for him to know how she felt about him, sure that the feelings were reciprocated. They were always flirting with one another. Granted, the flirting was never extreme, but it was there. She would catch him gazing at her at times. Plus, she had adored his mother. She thought about the times she had spent with her before her death. The woman was a joy to be around. It had been almost a year since his mother, Donna, had passed away due to cancer. She felt a stab of pain in her chest. Her heart hurt for him. His mother's death had hit him very hard.

She'd tried to be there as much as she could for him back then.

Well, all of that was in the past. Eric seemed to be healing quite well. He still didn't smile or laugh as much as he used to, but at least he had started back hanging out with his friends and just interacting in general.

Kat remembered calling him one night because she could not stop thinking about him. That night, she listened to him cry and pour out his heart to her. He had been drinking and his wound was still raw. She had stayed on the phone with him that entire night; stayed on the phone until he passed out without hanging up. The next day at work, he approached her and thanked her for listening to him, just for being there and she thought they were working their way back from the embarrassing outburst.

She did not know why she could not get him off her mind. It seemed as if they were supposed to be together. She did know that she needed to get herself together and let go of that simple schoolgirl crush and act like a grown-ass woman. He did not feel the same way. He would always see her as a coworker of his that his mom had befriended.

Kat shook her head to clear out all of the cobwebs and focused on her work. There would be a meeting in a few hours and she knew that she needed to be prepared for it or else the Queen Bitch would harass her first. Even though her workload for that day was heavy, she still caught herself looking in Eric's direction. After what seemed like the millionth time, she glanced around the room. When her eyes fell upon Christy, she saw her friend smirking at her. Kat shook her head and turned her attention back to her computer screen. Eric was going to be the reason she ended up in the unemployment line if she wasn't careful.

CHAPTER 4

ANGELA WALKED around the room. "Look, I know you guys want to go home, but we need to get this editing done ASAP. It needs to be done by tomorrow morning and not a moment later. I know you guys think I am always asking for a lot, so I am going to approach this from a different angle this time." She eyed the employees sitting around the conference table. "Before I start assigning people, I'm going to ask for volunteers. If I get enough of them, then I won't have to force anyone to volunteer their time."

Kat really did love her job; she just didn't like the early mornings and some of the people she worked with. So she was the first one to raise her hand.

"Someone doesn't have a life," Mark whispered to Eric loud enough to be heard by others. Kat heard a few people snickering at his comment. She didn't care. She had a house and future children to make money for. They could laugh all they wanted as long as she got hers.

"Someone won't have a job tomorrow if I hear another stupid-ass remark like that," Angela said, her eyes throwing daggers in Mark's direction. "Now, all we need are two more and the rest of you will be free to go. And, Mark, if I don't get my two, you will be my first pick. So get ready."

Eric said, "I'm in."

"Man, are you crazy?" Mark asked. "We are supposed to go to that new club on Chestnut Expressway tonight, remember?" His look spoke volumes. Kat knew he needed Eric to go so that he could get all of Eric's rejects.

Eric waved one hand. "Yeah, but I don't really feel like hanging out tonight. Plus, I could use the extra money."

"Use the extra money for what? You don't spend any money, with your cheap ass," Alex chimed in from across the table.

Everyone knew Eric was from money. Donna and her husband had made some great investments in their time and both had left it all to him. It was known that he didn't want for anything at all, but he still chose to come in every day. He wanted to make his own mark in the world without his parent's hard earned money.

"Ha ha. Get out of my business," Eric warned both of his boys. They closed their mouths instantly. He was a force to be reckoned with when upset and they both knew it as well as everyone else in the office.

"Good, now we only need one more person," Angela said as she wrote on a notepad.

"I would also like to help."

Kat turned to see who had spoken. It was the new chick named Trixie. She had that stereotypical ghetto-girl look. She wore a blonde lace front wig and a ton of makeup. She had a much lighter skin tone than Kat, who could not understand why she chose to paint her face like that. Trixie was a little on the short side, maybe 5'1, and she had a huge butt that the guys loved looking at.

The other woman was always smacking on gum and Kat found that to be downright irritating at times. The clothing that she wore always fit like a second skin. Kat guessed that she probably suffered from frequent yeast infections because her shit was always tight. Other than all of that, she didn't really know much about her, just that she had been on the job less than three months, had three kids, and had already slept with five dudes in the office. Kat kept her distance because it seemed like Trixie might have a little drama associated with her and Kat was good on that.

She knew that she didn't have the right to pass judgment and she knew her dislike of the woman had to do mainly with jealousy because of Eric. Shit, she knew why the newbie had volunteered. So did most of the people in the meeting with them. She had a thing for Eric as most women did. Kat couldn't blame her at all, because he had to be one of the most gorgeous men that she had ever seen in her life. One of the most delicious men to ever walk the face of the earth. He stood around 6'2 and had piercing gray eyes that seemed to look into one's soul. His style was always professional; even on the dress down days he looked like he was in charge. He carried an air of confidence with him at all times. He wasn't loud or boisterous like his friends. When he smiled, the room lit up. He had a beautiful smile with straight white teeth, but it had become almost nonexistent after the passing of his mother. There was a sadness about him that Kat could sense. She thought that was why her feelings for him wouldn't completely leave. They were always there just beneath the surface, threatening to make themselves known.

Trixie seemed to appreciate his looks the same as everyone else. Kat didn't quite know if it was mutual, but she had seen them flirting with one another from time to time. That shit pissed her off big time. It made her wonder what was really wrong with her. She thought that she was an okay person. Granted, she didn't dress like a video vixen, she tended to lean more toward the conservative look. She guessed to some men that meant that she might be a bore in the bedroom. She was not loud and she didn't talk much, so some might say that she was shy, which was true, but just not to the extreme. She definitely didn't have a supermodel's shape. She was more on the well-endowed side. She was a little self-conscious about her size, so she tended to keep it covered. But not in a bad way, like she was not stylish. Kat considered herself to be stylish with some class. Just like the true southern belle that her mama raised her to be.

With their combined efforts, the extra work did not take quite as long as Kat thought it would. No one spoke as they all put in work. In the end, it all paid off wonderfully. Well, the others were busy working, while Miss Trixie made subtle passes at Eric, trying to get him to go home with her.

Kat tried not to pay attention to it, but she could not help herself. Yes, she was feeling a little bit jealous. She couldn't help it, nor could she control her feelings for Eric. He accepted

Trixie's advances, whereas he had shot Kat's down. She guessed he was not into women her size or something. She did not know, but she did know that she was tired of trying to figure out what it was about her that he did not like. It was time to move on with her life and forget about him with his fine ass.

It was around eight that night when they finally put the finishing touches on the project. Trixie asked Eric if he could give her a ride home. He glanced at Kat before he answered and Kat was feeling some type of way because of it. She had noticed him throwing looks her way the whole time. Maybe he was letting her know that Trixie was the kind of chick that he could get down with. Whatever, she thought.

CHAPTER 5

KAT WENT to her desk to gather her belongings before heading home. Angela knocked on the outside of the cubicle. It did not surprise Kat one bit when she did not wait for an invitation before walking around to Kat's side.

She thinks she is the shit, Kat thought.

"Thanks so much for the help, Kat. I really appreciate the work you put in tonight. I think we just might be ahead of our projects for this week." Angela made her way to one of the chairs next to Kat's desk.

"It's no problem. I really enjoy the work and I love the overtime pay that it brings." Kat chuckled a little. Her salary was nice, but the overtime made it very lovely.

She had just purchased a house right outside of the city limits. It was a fixer-upper, a little project that she had decided to take on. The house was a two-story, old Victorian home. Her family thought that she was insane for buying it, but it was her money that paid for it and she worked hard for it. She knew that it would be gorgeous once it was completed. The yard was marvelous; it was her pride and joy. Kat had a lovely Koi pond in the back. She had added a gazebo and she was thinking of adding a pool. Gardening was her hobby. She had done a lot of work on her yard. She wanted to add a vegetable garden in the back. She knew that she would get it all done eventually.

"That is nice to know. The next time I need someone for overtime, I am going to automatically sign your ass up," Angela joked. At least Kat hoped she was.

"You have let me know ahead of time," Kat informed her with a stern expression on her face.

"Sure, I can do that. Boy, I am tired. I need something sweet to eat ASAP." The last part she said more to herself than to me.

"I have some chocolate in my desk. You are welcome to some if you like," Kat told her, thinking that she had a sweet tooth like she did.

"Oh, I am sure you don't have the kind of sweets I need. Well, you do, but just not in your desk." The look in her eyes challenged Kat to ask her what she meant.

Instantly, Kat felt some type of way. She didn't bite the bait right then. She chose to play it off, thinking that maybe she had read Angela wrong.

"I have a variety in here. You can look and see if anything appeals to you," Kat told her. She didn't know why, but she felt a different sort of energy flowing through the room. She admitted to herself that she was enjoying it.

Angela walked around the desk and leaned over Kat to look in the drawer. She could have easily walked on the other side of Kat, she did not. As she leaned over Kat, her arm grazed Kat's breast ever so slightly. Kat's nipple puckered up at contact.

Damn, Kat thought that she had to have been tripping. She had never considered herself to be a lesbian, not even bisexual, but the sexual tension was increasing by the second.

"Hmmm, I don't see anything in here to satisfy my appetite," Angela said as she straightened up. She did not move, stood right in that spot looking down at Kat.

Kat sat back in her chair and let her thoughts run rampant in her head before choosing how to reply. "Is there anything at all in here that you desire?"

Angela pushed Kat's chair back a little and stood directly in front of her. "Yes, there is. Can I have it?"

"Tell me what it is and I will see if it is on the market."

"I can show you better than I can tell you." She lowered herself to her knees and placed her hands on Kat's knees.

"What is it that you want, Angela?" Kat was not gullible; she just wanted to hear her say the words.

"I want to taste you." Angela let her fingers graze over Kat's flesh before letting them travel underneath her skirt. She looked at Kat, waiting for permission to proceed.

Kat did not give it to her. Instead she sat there looking, waiting for Angela to take what she wanted. She had no intention of stopping her, but she was not going to verbalize it either.

Angela gave a small smile, lowered her head, and kissed the inside of Kat's thigh. It was just a slight brush of her lips, but it sent a sensation straight to Kat's pussy and she jumped a little from the feeling. Angela's eyes met hers right before she placed another kiss on her thigh. This one was further up and a little longer. That kiss made Kat gasp just a little.

"Have you ever been with a woman?"

"No."

"Let me show you what it's like. I promise that you won't be disappointed. I can give you an orgasm like you have never experienced before. I can make you cum over and over again." While she was talking, her breath was caressing Kat's legs, sending electric shocks all through her body. She did not wait for her to answer.

Angela pushed Kat's skirt up and pulled her panties off. Then she placed each leg on the arm of the chair. She took her time inspecting Kat's hidden treasure.

Kat saw the lust in her eyes. She suddenly felt bold. "Now do you see something you want?" Her pussy was very wet and ready for contact. She was a little nervous, but she wanted that orgasm more.

"Oh yes, I do. Some sweet chocolate." Her tongue swept across her lips.

The wait was killing Kat ever so slowly. "Angela…" She was tempted to beg the other woman to give her what she craved.

Finally, after a minute, she started to devour Kat. Her mouth covered Kat's pussy in full. Her delightful pink tongue was stroking so many places that Kat couldn't think straight. Angela put her hands underneath Kat's ass and lifted her pussy up for more access and continued to feast like she was starving. Over and over, she sucked and licked on Kat's clit until she begged her to stop.

Not because it wasn't good, but because the pleasure was immense. It was beyond what Kat had expected. Damn, this woman just ate my pussy better than any man that I've ever been with, Kat thought. Her chair was soaked with cum and her legs were trembling just a little.

"Did you enjoy it?" Angela licked her lips, her eyes still on Kat's pussy.

"Yes," Kat admitted.

Angela's hands came up and began to fondle Kat's breasts. "Damn, Kat, I need more, baby." She rose up and suckled one nipple and twirled the other between her fingers. "You taste so fucking sweet. I always knew you would." She admitted to fantasizing of having Kat in this particular position before. "Come home with me, baby?"

There was no need for her to ask. Kat was willing to follow her ass anywhere as long as she kept making her cum like that.

Once they arrived at her house, with Kat following her, Angela did not hesitate to pick up where they had left off. The only difference was that in her bed, she had more access to Kat's body. There were no clothes in her way, nothing stopping her from getting all that she wanted from Kat. By the time she was done, Kat couldn't speak, couldn't think, couldn't really do shit but pass the hell out in her arms.

Kat woke up to Angela arms wrapped around her body. That was a blissful rest, the best that Kat had in a long time. Granted, she had to get up a little earlier to go home and get dressed for work, but it was well worth it, because Angela serviced her one more time before she departed. Kat swore that she had never been with anyone that had so much sexual energy. Angela was always ready for it and Kat was open to receive it all. That night was the first time that she actually tasted another woman's juices, and she discovered that she really enjoyed the taste. Angela was more of a giver than receiver and Kat did not mind it one bit. As Kat was leaving, they shared a passionate kiss with promises of more to come.

CHAPTER 6

KAT WAS nervous as she approached her job. She didn't quite know how to act around Angela in the daylight or what to expect from her, so her nerves were all over the place. The day went by smoothly and without incident. They both carried on in their usual ways in the office. Toward the end of the day, Angela sent Kat a message on her computer saying that she had a great time and asking if Kat would like to hang out with her that night.

Hmmm… Kat thought for a minute. Hell yes, she wanted that. She thought that she must be a lesbian because she was feeling that woman. Kat had literally been thinking of Angela and her tongue all damn day. Every time a thought crossed her mind, she became moist. Luckily, she kept wipes in her desk. She was so not feeling walking around the entire day with damp-ass panties. They agreed on dinner at Kat's place with dessert afterwards. As Kat was leaving her office heading to the elevator, Eric crossed her path.

"Hello, Kat. How are you?" He greeted her in a professional manner. She was so sick of the way he spoke to her. It was as if they were complete strangers. She brushed that feeling to the side and turned towards him.

"Hi there, I'm good. How are you?" Any other time, she would have been nervous by his approach, but on this day, Kat was in the zone and ready for her date with Angela and her oh-so-fabulous tongue.

"I can't complain," he told her while holding his hands out in a surrender gesture.

"It never does any good anyways," Kat joked with him.

"That's so true. You are looking very beautiful today," he said, seeming to appraise her from head to toe.

"Thank you very much for that." She wondered where all of this was coming from.

"Do you have a new man or something?" he asked her while still looking her up and down.

"No, why would you ask that?" Kat was intrigued.

"Nothing, it's just that you have this glow about you that I haven't seen before and it looks lovely on you." His adorable gray eyes seemed to hold interest, like he wanted to prolong the conversation, but she was in a rush. She had to get prepared for a night of complete ecstasy with Angela and her long-ass tongue, but he definitely did not need to know all of that.

"Thanks very much." Kat smiled as she stepped onto the elevator with him following. She didn't know how, but she could feel his eyes on her ass. She turned around slowly, giving him time to check out all that he had passed up. He wasn't shy by a long shot. She watched as his eyes took their time in making their way back up to hers.

"Are you going to Jayden's tonight?"

Jayden's was a club/bar that a lot of the coworkers met up at after work for drinks. It was not an everyday thing, but it was fun sometimes. Kat often indulged in the activity just to mingle with others and because Christy always begged her to go.

"No, not tonight. I have plans." Her mind drifted back to Angela's bedroom. Just that quick, she was lost in a fantasy of Angela's lips on hers. She had to catch herself because she thought that she may have moaned slightly. The way that he was looking at her confirmed her suspicion.

"So it's like that?" he asked. His eyes were lowered.

"Like what?" she feigned ignorance. She knew what he meant.

"Whoever you are going to meet has you gone like that? You're glowing, gazing and I think I heard you make a moaning sound," he said.

Slightly embarrassed for moaning out loud, she looked straight ahead and said. "It's possible." She giggled a little, feeling like a silly school girl.

"I guess I missed my opportunity, huh," he stated rather than asking her.

That threw Kat for a loop. He could not possibly be saying things like that now that she was involved with someone. Hell yeah, you missed your shot, was the thought that ran across her mind. She wanted to curse his ass out for real. That "better late than never" crap was so damn played out. She decided that she didn't need his ass trying to rain on her rainbow parade.

She looked at him and smirked. She had better things to do than sit around and wait for him to decide if she was worthy of his damn time. Screw him. Even though now, he made her feel sexy, like a goddess even. She felt that familiar pull in her stomach as the elevators finally opened to the bottom floor. Kat made the conscious decision to throw her hips a little more as she walked out, to really give him something to look at. She felt powerful as she strolled along ahead of him, but then she stopped, and turned to him with a question about work.

After a brief chat, Kat was living in the moment and Eric was checking her out like he appreciated what he saw. Her heart skipped a few beats and she held her head high while he walked her to her car. She already felt simply delightful after the night she spent with Angela. His attention was the icing on the cake. Her day was going marvelous for once and she was going to enjoy the hell out of it.

CHAPTER 7

ERIC COULD not believe how delicious Kat looked and how her ass jiggled as she walked. The skirt she had on was fitted snuggly across her voluptuous ass, and every time she took a step, the fabric moved with her rhythm. He could not take his eyes off her and he had a feeling that she knew it. He had never taken her to be a hellcat. He was beginning to learn otherwise. The elevator arrived at their destination much sooner than he would have preferred. He let her step off first then followed in her wake, eyes still glued to her rear. She stopped suddenly and turned toward him and caught him in the act. He felt his temperature rising. Hell, he was feeling a little embarrassed by her catching him. That look in her eyes let him know that he'd better watch himself.

"I wanted to know if we needed to get together this weekend to go over that proposal. Or do you feel confident with the work already?" She got right down to business. She had to know that his mind was else places because it took him a minute to reply.

"Umm … I, umm, yes. I think we should at least go over it again before turning it in on Monday." He cleared his throat, knowing that the proposal was damn near perfect. He was just using it as an excuse to see her this weekend.

"Okay, so where would you like to meet up, my place or yours? Or we can go to a restaurant if you prefer?"

Jackpot, he thought. "I'm good. We can meet at your place. I can stop by after I leave the gym. It's on my way home." Yes, he did let her get away, but he was no longer delusional. He wanted this woman and he was willing to do whatever it took to get her. Even if it meant playing dirty and trying to seduce her on her own turf. He was in it to win it.

"Sunday evening around five is good for me. That way we can have most of our weekend still free. It should only take about an hour to get it done. How is that for you?" She was all business. He knew he had his work cut out for him. He had to move that damn mountain that he had allowed her to build where he was concerned.

"That's great actually. I should be leaving the gym around that time. I can even grab us a bite to eat before I stop by." He knew he was pushing, but oh well.

"You don't have to go to any trouble."

"It's okay. We all need sustenance to survive. And you know that all of that paperwork drains the hell out of you like everyone else. Stop trying to pretend that you love this crap. Come on, be honest with me." He elbowed her in the side.

Kat couldn't contain her laughter. She disliked going over proposals just like the next person. "Alright, you got me. It does absorb all of my energy and I probably will require food."

"That's what I'm talking about." Eric threw an arm around

her shoulder and walked her to her car.

This was the first time that he had made physical contact with her outside of a handshake. He admitted to himself that it felt nice.

Once they had arrived to her car, he opened her door for her. "I hope you have fun on your date tonight." He was fishing for information, but she gave him none.

"I'm planning on it," she answered with a twinkle in her eyes. She climbed in her car and waved as she drove off.

Eric stood there wondering who this mystery person was who had taken her attention and affection from him. He wanted it all back. Kat was his dream woman and he was ready and willing to fight for her.

On the drive home, Kat's mind drifted to Eric and their brief exchange. He seemed different today. She was thrown off guard by his act of kindness. He was always so formal with her. She didn't know how to take this behavior. She wasn't sure the reason for it, but his actions had her wondering what if he was up to something.

Men and their damn baggage, she thought as she hurried home to get ready for her night with Angela.

CHAPTER 8

ERIC KNEW that he should have stayed home. One of these days, he was going to actually pay attention to that little voice when it gives him advice. Jayden's was packed to the gill. The freaks were out hard. He wanted to get lost in the music, have a few drinks, and maybe take some lucky lady home to get his mind off of Kat and her new man.

As soon as he claimed a spot at the bar, the women started flocking. It was always like that for him. He never had to work hard to get a female's number. His boys blamed it all on his gray eyes, but he knew it was because of his confidence and his swag. Women were intrigued by his eyes, but his style and his deep baritone voice had all the ladies hooked. His friends called him a tad bit conceited. He didn't see anything wrong with wanting to look good. His mission was always dress to impress. First impressions were everything to him.

As he sat there, his mind started drifting back to work and Kat. He wondered if she was having fun on her date. A woman standing next to him leaned in and asked if he would like a drink. He took in her demeanor and clothes and accepted her offer. She was a very gorgeous woman. He leaned back a little and looked at her long legs that led up to a nice, round behind. He assumed that was the reason she chose to stand, to make sure all the brothers got a look at the nice view.

"What are your plans for tonight?" she asked him.

"What would you like for them to be?" His eyes twinkled in anticipation of a night between her long legs.

"I think you should come home with me and let me make you feel like a man is supposed to feel." Her voice had a little squeak that Eric had begun to find annoying just that quick.

"Is that right? The night is still young, anything is possible."

"We should think about making it an early night, if you know what I mean."

He knew what she meant. But that voice was an absolute turn off and he was no longer feeling her. She should say less as possible, he thought.

He looked around the room trying to spot someone familiar. She got bold and let her hands wander along his thigh. "Umm, nice and firm. I like that," she squealed.

He eased her hand off of his leg. The urge to have a night of uninhibited sex no longer appealed to him. He just wanted her to move on.

Even though he tried not to, he wondered how Kat was making out on her date. He wished that he was the one making her glow with happiness. If only he hadn't said all of those horrible things to her. An apology might have made things a little better, but he didn't even have the courage to do that. It seemed best to act like it didn't happen. Even though he wished it hadn't, every time he looked in her eyes it reminded him that it did and there was no going back or do overs.

"Is your lady here?" The woman's voice sounded like plastic rain boots rubbing together and it was giving him a headache.

"No, I'm single." Shit, he should not have said that. Now he was going to have a harder time getting rid of her.

"Woo, that's nice to know. I'm single too." Her smile was anything but innocent.

"And just why are you single, little lady?" Eric turned toward her to let her know she had his attention finally.

He had made up his mind, he was going home alone, but he didn't have to be rude to her. His mission was to get his woman. Kat was the only one for him, he knew it and so did his mother, God rest her soul. His mother adored Kat. She had given him her blessings before she passed. She was the only other person who knew his true feelings for Kat besides Tim, his best friend. Eric probably would have been with Kat right now if things had not worked out the way they did. He'd had a thing for her for almost a year. His mother, Donna, thought it was cute the way his face would light up when he talked about Kat. Donna fell in love with Kat at a company picnic that her son had brought her to. She'd spent most of the time getting to know the young lady who had stolen her son's heart and she was not disappointed.

Bad timing was the problem when Kat had approached Eric. He was in a bad place. He had just learned of his mother's cancer and that she only had a few months to live. Of course, she did not know that was the reason for his harsh words. He'd confided in his mother about the way he had treated Kat. Donna had told him to come clean with Kat about that day and just simply apologize. She told him that Kat would understand, but he was in his own feelings and didn't think it was a great time to entertain the thought of a relationship. He was losing his mother, his rock. He was not good for anything or anyone at that time. All he could do at that time was try and be strong for his mom. Now that he had finally begun to heal, and his feelings for Kat started to resurface and he now wanted to pursue her.

As predicted, he went home alone. The lady with the high pitched voice squeaked one too many times for him and he excused himself from her clutches and exited the club without glancing back in her direction. That night, he was plagued with thoughts of Kat and making love to her. He'd had so many dreams of her that he felt like he knew her body as well as he knew his own.

Finally home alone, he decided just to turn in. With thoughts of Kat dancing around in his head, he fell into a deep sleep. He jumped up from his bed to take a cold shower. He had to get a handle on his situation. He had to get this woman before it was too late and some other brother claimed her. He could not let that happen.

Kat was meant to be with him and he had to do whatever was necessary to convince her of it and show her just how good they could be together. He prayed that she would allow him the opportunity to prove himself to her. He'd hoped she'd forgive him for speaking to her in such a disrespectful and cruel way. He went back to bed with a game plan to revive her old feelings. Hopefully, she still had room in her heart for him.

CHAPTER 9

ANGELA RUSHED around her apartment getting ready for her date. She could not believe her luck. She never would have guessed that Kat was into women and was thrilled that she acted on instinct.

Their date was supposed to be casual, so she chose a pair of skintight jeans to wear. She knew her body was banging. Men were always coming on to her, trying to get some of her honey. She thought most of their efforts were somewhat amusing. She was a lesbian to the fullest and did not desire men at all. Most people didn't know that about her and she preferred it that way. But now, with Kat, maybe she could live her life out in the open.

She arrived at Kat's house an hour later. When she knocked on the door, she heard Kat tell her to come in. This was the first time she had been to her house. She took her time inspecting the décor. The living room had a relaxed atmosphere. It was obvious that Kat had a thing for plants. She had greenery everywhere.

"Would you like something to drink?" Kat asked as she entered the room.

Angela turned and let her eyes roam over Kat's frame before answering. "Sure, that would be great. You look stunning."

"Thank you," Kat said and headed into the kitchen to get her a drink.

And that was the truth. Kat had her hair straightened and hanging to her shoulders. She was the opposite of Angela. She wore a maxi dress with a pair of sandal heels. Her makeup was minimal. Angela couldn't recall ever seeing her in an overabundance amount of face paint. She was a natural beauty.

"I have white and red wine. Which do you prefer?" Kat called out from the kitchen.

Angela made her way to the kitchen. "Surprise me."

"I can do that," Kat said as she grabbed a couple of wine glasses from the cabinet. She poured the wine and handed a glass to Angela. "Do you want to listen to some music?" She seemed nervous.

Angela took a sip of her wine and set the glass on the counter. Then she walked over to Kat and took her glass from her hand.

"I've been thinking about your sweet lips all day." She drew Kat into her arms and took the kiss that she had been craving for the past nine hours.

"Is that the only thing you were thinking of?" Kat asked.

"No, definitely not," Angela murmured. "Show me to your bedroom and I will show you each and every thought that crossed my mind today." Her lips had found their way to Kat's neck and she nibbles lightly. Kat's head fell to the side. Angela chuckled. "You like that?"

"YES, you know I do," Kat moaned. She couldn't believe how this woman was turning her on. She felt a throbbing sensation between her legs and willed Angela to touch her there. Mental telepathy had never interest her, but she wished that she had it now.

"What would you like Kat?" Angela asked as her hands trailed down Kat's body.

"That," Kat said, letting her know that she was on the right path.

Angela leaned down and grazed her nipple through her dress. It didn't take long for them to undress and get into Kat's bed.

In Kat's mind, Eric's face replaced Angela's. Kat closed her eyes and her body came alive. She knew that she was wrong for wishing it was him doing all of those things to her, but she could not stop the images from entering her brain. Her orgasm was intense, very intense. She saw him sucking on her pussy instead of Angela. It was his fingers inside her, stroking her G-spot. When she came, it was powerful. In her mind, it was Eric who licked up all of her juices.

It was Eric in her heart.

The next evening, after she convinced Angela to leave, Kat ran herself a hot bubble bath and added her favorite apple scented bubble bath to the flowing water. She turned the lights down low, lit a few candles, and put a R. Kelly CD in to groove to while she relaxed.

She eased her body into the hot water, closed her eyes, and let it consume her. A vivid image of Eric dancing with her played in her head like it was on a giant movie screen.

He looked at her as if she was the most desirable woman

in the world. His hands were on her lower back just above her butt. She mentally begged him to let them slide further down and explore her body. His eyes told her that he knew what she wanted and that he was more than happy to grant her wish. Kat's heart thudded in her chest. His gaze fell to her lips and his desire to taste them was evident. She whimpered slightly as he lowered his mouth to hers.

The ringing of her phone snapped Kat out of the fantasy yet again. She swore under her breath. Every single time she let her imagination run wild with thoughts of Eric, something or someone always interrupted. Maybe it was a sign that they did not belong together. She shook her head and climbed out of the tub so ready to give the caller an ear full that she didn't even check the caller ID.

"Hello?" She let the irritation be heard over the line.

"I'm sorry, did I catch you at a bad time?"

Kat thought her mind was playing some sort of trick on her. The voice had the same owner as the one in her fantasy. She cleared her throat before speaking. "Ummm, no... I'm sorry, I thought you were someone else, a telemarketer or something."

"I just wanted to make sure we were still on for tomorrow." Eric said.

"Yeah, sure we are, unless you have something else to do. If you are busy, it's okay, we can just go over it Monday morning." She knew she was rambling.

"Oh no, I made sure I kept Sunday open for you. I will be there on time. Or would you rather I stop by there tonight?" His tone indicated that work was not on his mind at the moment.

Kat was speechless. Was he coming on to her? She shook her head, quickly erasing it as a figment of her imagination. "No need to come by tonight. Sunday will be fine." If he came over now, she was liable to jump his bones.

"Okay, you can't say that I didn't try." He chuckled. "I will see you on tomorrow. Have a pleasant dream tonight."

"You too," Kat whispered before disconnecting the call.

She leaned against the wall to keep from falling, amazed that he called at the same time she was thinking of him. She knew it had to be fate or something like that. As much as she wanted to believe that he wanted more, self-doubt worked its way into her mind, reminding her of his rejection of her.

She shook it off and went back up and let the water out of the tub and got dressed for bed.

Sleep did not come easily for her that night. All she could think of was Eric and his piercing gray eyes raking over her nude body.

CHAPTER 10

KAT COULD not believe her luck. Her sister got called in to work at the last minute and had begged her to keep her three kids. The kids would be a great reason to call Eric and cancel their meeting. She had a great time with Angela and she knew that Eric would have questions, maybe even look at her funny and learn her secret. She grabbed her phone to call him.

"Hey Eric," she said as soon as he picked up. "I'm sorry, but something came up. I'm babysitting for my sister. Can you get someone else to go over the proposal with you? Or maybe we can do it early in the morning? Because I am sure we probably will not get much work done with the kids running around."

Eric did not say anything for a moment. "Are you sure you aren't just trying to get rid of me?"

"Umm … no. Why would you think that?"

"Yeah sure. Hey, I am good with kids. I don't mind at all."

"You like kids?" Kat was surprised.

"Yes, I love kids. I want a big family one day," he confided to her.

"And just how many?" Kat's eyes bucked.

"Three or four. I have always wanted a lot of children."

"Wow, I would not have guessed that."

"Most people wouldn't. They just think of me as a playboy. You know, the ultimate bachelor." He laughed at his own words.

"Well, if you are sure that it will not bother you…"

"It won't, I am good. I will be there at five on the dot. Oh, and Kat?"

"Yes?"

"Nice try."

ERIC hung the phone up and smiled to himself. He knew Kat was trying to get out of meeting him and he knew why. She still wanted him. Checkmate.

ERIC came over with pizza and Chinese. The kids loved him and he them. It was like a mini party to them. He played video games with the oldest boy and dolls with the girl. He even spent time playing with the baby. He was great with them and Kat took notice of everything. It all seemed genuine. He seemed so different outside of the office. She caught herself wondering if this was how it would be if they had gotten together and had kids. Deep down she knew that was farfetched, so she decided to curb her thoughts.

Shit, she had just had a sexual session with a woman between her legs whispering words of love to her. Now, here he was showing her a side of him that had her interested even more. She knew that she said she was done, but damn, he had her curious. Was he really marriage material? Did he really want to be a father?

When it was time for the kids to go, she had to pick up a sleeping baby boy off the chest of a sleeping Eric. The sight was so cute that she just had to snap a picture.

After the children had left, the two adults got to work. The doorbell sounded when they were halfway done. Kat opened the door, and to her surprise, Angela stood on the other side.

"Hi baby, how are you?" Angela said as she stepped inside.

"Angela, how are you?" Eric greeted her as she approached the kitchen table.

"I am great. What are you two doing?"

"We are just finishing up the Sudsy proposal."

Eric put his head down and continued to go over the last of the papers. He had no reason to suspect a thing, but that didn't ease Kat's nerves. She just knew that he could see Angela's visit for what it really was.

"Oh, that is great." Just that quick, Angela went into Queen Bitch mode. "Maybe I can go ahead and take it with me when I leave." She looked over at Kat and motioned for her to join her in the other room. "Eric, please excuse us for a minute. I need to speak with Angela."

In the privacy of Kat's spare room, Angela pushed her against the wall and devoured her mouth. "Why is he here?" she asked finally.

"He just told you that we are working." Kat wasn't quite sure why Angela's kisses were irritating her when the day before they had her soaking wet.

"Yeah, but you guys can do that in the office. What is he doing here at your house?"

"This is how we chose to do it. I don't see why it would be a problem." Kat took a few steps back from Angela. She took in the woman's demeanor. What she saw was not attractive in the least bit.

"You were in love with him." Angela sneered. "Yeah, it is a big problem."

Kat regretted opening the door for her boss. "That is all in the past. You know, just like everyone else, the way he turned me down and humiliated me." Kat could not believe that she was explaining herself to Angela. It was not as if they were in a committed relationship or if she and Eric were attempting to have one. Hell, all they were doing was fucking working. Off the clock at that. "I do not see why it is any of your business anyway."

"Oh really? Yes, it is my business. It became that once you allowed me access to your pussy. It then became mine."

"Angela, don't you think I would have to be in agreement with you for that to be true?"

"It became true when you gave it to me repeatedly."

"Look, we are just working. This right here, what you are doing, is a little extreme. If this is the way it's going to be, then let's just stop it right here. I am no one's property. I am my own woman." Kat did enjoy spending time with Angela, but she did not know how she felt about being in a lesbian relationship and it wasn't right to string her along.

"I apologize. It is just that I am really feeling you and I want more. I want a relationship with you." Angela leaned toward Kat.

Kat stopped her before their lips made contact. "I have company. It is rude to leave company alone for a great deal of time, you know that."

"Oh okay, fine. I will leave you to your company." She left the room and Kat followed her to the kitchen. "So, Eric, is the proposal good? Can I take it with me now?"

"Uh, no," Eric said, "we still have a little more to go over. It should be done in about an hour. I can drop it off first thing in the morning if you like."

"Okay, that will be fine. I guess I will see you guys in the morning. Sorry for interrupting your company, Kat. I just wanted to drop by. If I hadda known you were working, I wouldn't have dropped in on you." Angela raised an eyebrow.

"It's no problem. Like Eric said, it will be ready in the morning." Kat read Angela's meaning. As she walked her to the door, she said, "I don't appreciate you trying to keep tabs on me or what I do."

"My bad for coming to see you. I wanted to surprise you, but I'm the one surprised. It's all good, though," Angela said as she walked out of the door.

Kat watched her as she got in her car and pulled off. She closed the door and returned to the kitchen to help Eric with the rest of the paperwork.

CHAPTER 11

AS SOON as Kat was seated, Eric said, "I didn't know you guys were on those terms. I thought she could not stand your ass." He frowned. "Did you tell her we were working today?"

Kat answered without thinking. "No, I didn't."

"Hmmm … I guess she just wanted to hang out?"

She smiled. "I guess, I don't know. She has never just dropped by before." Kat didn't want him to be suspicious of her and Angela's relationship.

They finished up around midnight. Kat knew she should call it a night, but she was enjoying Eric's company and she didn't want him to go. Instead of bidding him good night, she asked if he wanted her to warm him up some food.

"Sure, that would be great." He didn't seem ready to leave. "That way, when I do get home, I can shower and crash. I am not a morning person. I have to force myself out of bed on most days."

"Oh my goodness, me too. I want to smash my alarm clock every morning for going off." They shared a laugh.

KAT prepared their plates and they continued with their conversation. Eric was happy they were having a pleasant time, especially after the incident at work and how he treated her. Spending the day with her, all of the old feelings that he thought he had buried along with his mother were still there.

"Today has been a lovely day. I had fun with the kids."

"They had fun too. They acted like they didn't want to leave you. And the next time they come over for a visit, they will be asking for you."

"Oh, that's cool. If they want to hang out with me, just call me and I'll come over." He thought about what he had said. He had just placed himself in her life without asking her permission. "Well, if that is okay with you, I mean."

"They would love that. Especially Rickie. He always wants to play those damn video games and auntie Kat don't have a clue. I play with him, but he beats the pants off of me each and every time." She shook her head.

"I know that's right. A little man after my own heart; he knows a good time when he sees it." Eric finished his food. He had tried eating slow to waste time, but it didn't work.

"I see you are done. Do you want more?" Kat asked.

"Sure, hook me up. Thanks for being so hospitable."

"Yeah, whatever. You bought the food, remember?" she reminded him.

"I know, but you are the one preparing the plates and warming the food. Plus, the company is great too." Her back was to him, so he took the opportunity to check her out from behind. He liked what he saw. He liked it a whole lot. He cleared his throat. "So," he said, "tell me about this mystery man."

"What do you mean?"

"You know, the man who has you glowing like that." He felt a slight ting of jealousy.

"My lips are sealed," she said.

"Awww, come on. I thought we were friends."

Kat turned around with her hands on her hips. "When did we become friends, Eric?"

"Today. At least, I thought we were on our way to being cool again. My bad, didn't mean to overstep my boundaries."

"It's cool. We are friends. I was just pulling your leg." She placed his plate on the table and sat back down.

"Aren't you having more?" He felt greedy, being that he was on his second plate. This time, he was going to take his time and eat at a slower pace.

"I'm good. You go ahead."

"I feel like a hog."

"Whatever. You are a guy and I know y'all be smashing food."

"True, I do like to eat." He licked his lips as an image of him buried between her legs entered his mind.

"I guess it's cool as long as you don't overdo it. Your body doesn't seem to suffer from it in any way. Me, on the other hand, I gain weight by looking at food, mostly in my thighs at that. I have some thunder thighs." She laughed.

Eric looked around the table at her legs that were covered in sweat pants. "Oh yeah? Stand up and let me see?" He asked her, knowing full well that he knew exactly what her thighs looked like.

"No can do," she said.

"Why not? I can tell you if I think they are 'thunder thighs' as you say."

"I don't care what you say; it is how I feel that matters."

"Okay, so if I said that I thought you were the most beautiful woman in the world and that I would love to be inside of your thighs, that wouldn't matter to you?"

Without blinking. "No it would not," she answered.

"Damn. Really?" He was shocked by her answer. He figured that she would have been blushing by now. "Why wouldn't it matter?"

"If it was said by someone else, then it might. But you, nope, it wouldn't."

"Wow, so I'm nobody?" His feelings were hurt by her answer.

"You are somebody. Somebody who's not into me. So when you say it, I know that you don't mean it. Whereas, with some other guy, it would be different, because they probably haven't humiliated me publicly."

Eric was stunned by what she said. He knew he had hurt her, but he didn't know just how much his words had affected her. "I've been meaning to talk to you about that. I'm so sorry for the way I treated you. I promise you that it was not my intentions to hurt you. It just came out that way." He saw her eyes water and he realized just how much damage his words had caused her. "Look, it was a bad time for me, a very bad time. I had just found out about my mother's health. The day before, the doctor had told us how much time she had left. I was in a lot of pain and in a very negative place. I wanted to everyone to hurt the way that I was hurting. I know that it wasn't right to take it out on you, but I did. It had nothing at all to do with you, just bad timing."

"I never knew that." Her voice held sincerity.

"How could you? Only a few people knew it. I was angry. I know it doesn't justify my actions, but I need for you to know that it was not because of you, or the way you look, or my feeling concerning you. I honestly can't say that I recall much that day except the look on your face afterwards. I wanted to stop you to apologize, but that anger would not allow me to." He looked down at his hands and let out a chuckle. "You want to hear something funny?"

"Sure," she said.

"My mom adored you. She said that you were like a breath of fresh air to her." He smiled as he recalled the conversations they had about Kat.

"Really? That is so sweet." Kat clutched her chest.

"She picked you for me," Eric admitted while looking Kat in the eyes.

"What do you mean?"

"She said that you would be my wife and the mother of my children, that you were her future daughter-in-law. She wanted me to know that she approved of you before she passed on." He looked down at his hands again. He felt vulnerable. He had never let another person see him so open before.

"Oh," was all Kat said.

He imagined she was at a loss for words with that news. He, too, was at a loss for words.

After a few minutes of silence he figured he just needed to leave. He stood and said that he was going to head home.

Kat walked him to the door. He turned to her and gazed at her for a moment before speaking.

"Thanks for today. I haven't had that much fun in a very long time. I really appreciate it and you."

"No problem, thank you also," she replied.

Eric paused before adding, "Thanks for being the light in my mother's eyes during her time of need. You brought joy to her. I never got a chance to tell you that either."

Kat smiled. "She was a joy to be around. I'm glad you feel that way. I'm glad that it mattered to her."

"It mattered more than you will ever know. And not only to her." He turned and walked out the door. Before getting into his car, he called out to her, "I will see you bright and early in the morning, my beautiful Kat."

Kat stood with her mouth open. Did Eric just call her his beautiful Kat?

CHAPTER 12

ON THE ride home, Eric replayed the day in his head. He knew Kat was the woman for him, he just had to make her see it. He vowed that, by that time next year, she would be on the way to becoming his wife. She did not know that before he found out about his mother's failing health, she held the priority spot in his mind. He remembered talking to his mom about her. She would sit and smile at him while he told her how beautiful his Kat was. He always had called her his when he spoke about her to his mom. That is why she had made it a mission to meet Kat. It was love at first sight for her.

Their company had sponsored a family day for the employees and Donna felt it was a great opportunity to meet this Kat person. Eric warned her to be on her best behavior since Kat didn't know how he felt. She just laughed and entered the picnic with every intention of finding out as much as she could about her future daughter-in-law.

The two women had been inseparable the entire afternoon. They spent time talking about all sorts of things. Kat listen as Donna told stories of her growing up. Stories of how she and Eric's father fell in love. She even shared stories of Eric as a child. Eric was amazed at how well they clicked. They even exchanged numbers for future lunch dates.

When he took his mother home, she admitted to him that she really liked Kat and that she wished them the best in life and love. He was surprised by it. She felt like not many women were good enough for her son, but Kat had made the cut with flying colors. He adored her just that much more.

His biggest problem was how to approach her. He was not a shy man by far, but this woman was special to him. He could not go to her with the same old weak crap that most men did. He had to be original and get her interested enough to want to date him. He had seen her shooting down advances left and right one night at Jayden's. She wasn't giving anybody any play. He wanted to make his move that night, but had talked himself out of it. He'd had a few drinks and let the opportunity pass. He still regretted his decision.

While plotting on how to make his approach, Donna became ill. She had known she was sick, but had kept it from him as long as she could. When it became evident, his life changed for the worst. He learned that his mother, his best friend, was slowly dying. She had been fighting all by herself.

At first, he was upset with her for not telling him, but she explained that she wanted to see him enjoying his life and not spending their last month's together grieving. He understood, but at the same time, he became angry with everyone. He felt like they were good people, so why were they being punished this way? His mother finally admitted to him that she was tired and she could no longer go on. She told him that she knew he would be okay, and she knew it to be so because Kat would see to it. She let him know that she thought he had made a great choice. She even stated that she thought Kat was his match, his soul mate. Just like his father had been hers.

Donna let him know that she missed her husband and she was ready to finally see him after all of those years. Eric listened and heard the pain in her heart that she had been keeping from him. He knew it was right for him to allow her to go. He also knew that she had held on as long as she did because of him. On that final day that he went to see her, got into bed with her, and held her.

"Mom, I love you so much," he told her. "You mean the world to me and I hate to lose you. I don't want you to go. I want you here with me for always. But I know that is selfish of me to feel this way. I know you are in pain and tired of the struggle, and I also know that you are ready to see Dad. You have sacrificed so much for me my whole life, and here I am being concerned about my needs and not being able to see you, to call you."

He let his tears flow freely as he held on to the shell of his mother. He felt her hands rub his arm. That let him know that she was listening. "All this time, I've been thinking of how I'm going to feel and all. I never once considered your feelings. I know that you love me. I am a grown man and I can provide for myself. You raised me well, Ma, so I am releasing you. Go on home, Momma. Go and be with Daddy and the rest of the family. I am no longer angry, Momma. You don't have to hang on any longer. It is okay, I will love you forever."

His mother smiled at him and spent her last evening telling him stories until he fell asleep by her side. When he awoke from his nap, he discovered that she had gone on to a better place. He felt an odd sense of peace while leaving the hospital. He knew in his heart that his parents were back together again.

The weeks following his mother's funeral were the hardest in his entire life. There were times when he wanted to end it all; he just wanted the pain to go away. He had started drinking heavily and alienating himself from his friends and extended family. He knew they were worried, but he didn't care. He was on a downward spiral until the night he opened up and confided to Kat. She stayed on the phone with him all night, or at least until he passed out, without once saying that she needed to go to bed or anything. Even after he never offered up an apology for treating her so bad. It felt good to get everything off his chest. He was able to evaluate his situation and turn things around for the better. She had helped him out more than she knew, more than he had expressed to her.

He made a vow to always be upfront with her concerning his feelings. He wanted more than a friendship, and he was going to work his ass off to make sure that he got more.

CHAPTER 13

Kat had just climbed into bed, ready for sleep to come, when she heard her phone ringing. She was tempted to ignore it, but curiosity got the best of her. Deep down, she hoped it was Eric. To her dismay, the caller ID showed it was Angela. She started not to answered, but for some reason she knew Angela would have kept on calling until she picked up.

"Hi, Angela," she said as soon as she answered.

"Is he still there?"

Kat ignored her question. "You do know that it is after midnight, right?"

"Yes, I know that. Is he still there?"

"Girl, it is late. Why would he still be here when we both have work in the morning? Or have you forgotten that fact?" Angela was beginning to piss her off with all of the questions.

"I know that. Like it really matters if you have work. If you want to have sex, then that is what you are going to do, regardless of the time."

"No, he is not here. He has been gone for a while. I am in bed. I have to work tomorrow. Good night." Kat hung up without waiting for Angela to reply. She had to set that chick straight as soon as possible.

After a night filled with dreams of Eric, she awoke the next day feeling different. Like new, revived for some reason. She didn't have any altercations with her alarm clock. In fact, she did not even hit the snooze button. She was excited to go to work for the first time in months. As she approached her desk, from the corner of her eye, she saw Eric watching her. She turned toward him and gave a slight wave. He returned the wave along with a bright smile. It made her feel warm all over.

All through the day, she caught him looking in her direction. He did not try to play it off. Instead, he smiled each time, confirming that he was indeed looking at her. She had never blushed so much in her entire life.

"So, what is up with all of the twitching around?" Christy asked Kat.

"I am just trying to get comfortable," she lied. She didn't want anyone in her business and trying to rain on her parade. She wanted to enjoy her secret flirting all by her lonesome. Yes, they were actually flirting. And she was definitely enjoying it.

"Yeah, okay. Tell me anything," her friend said as she continued with her paperwork.

"You need help with that?" Kat asked knowing that if she didn't, Christy would be staying late to get it done.

"Girl, yes. I need all of the help I can get. I swear editing is not my thing. I don't know why Angela always forces this crap on me." Kat remained silent. "What's up with you? First, it was all of the fidgeting, and now you are not even hating on Angela with me. Come clean. What happened this weekend?" She gave Kat all of her attention.

"Nothing. I am just in a good mood and I don't want to taint it with any negative thoughts. I just want to be happy today, that is all."

Turning back to her computer, she noticed an IM from Eric.

You are looking very beautiful today. I cannot keep my eyes off you and I do not want to either.

She felt herself blushing all over again. She immediately typed him a message.

I am glad that you are enjoying my radiance. Thanks for the compliment. You are looking mighty delicious yourself.

Her PC dinged, letting her know he had replied.

Delicious, huh? Would you care for a sample of something delicious? I mean, would you like to have dinner with me and we can go for some delicious food.

She laughed. She caught his meaning and she was definitely interested in sampling his goods.

I would love to have dinner with you.

Where would you like to go?"

Surprise me.

Kat had forgotten all about helping Christy. Eric had all of her attention.

I can do that. I will be over to pick you up around six thirty, okay?

Great, I can't wait.

Which was the truth. She was ready to leave work and go prepare for her date with him. She was amazed at how things were turning out. Just a few weeks ago, she was complaining about being lonely, and now she had two very sexy people interested in her. She knew she could not have both, but she would deal with that later. Tonight, she was going to focus on enjoying her evening out with Eric. She had been waiting on this moment for so long that it seemed surreal to her. The man of her dreams had just asked her out on a date. And he finally apologized and explained why he was so mean to her. She was elated.

Right before it was time to go home, she saw a delivery guy enter with flowers, a teddy bear, and two balloons. Whoever is getting that is one lucky woman, she thought. Nobody had ever sent her flowers before. She wondered how it felt to have someone that interested, then turned her attention back to her work.

"Excuse me, are you Kat?"

She turned and saw that it was the delivery guy. "Um, yes I'm Kat." He couldn't possibly be here for her, could he?

"These are for you." He handed her the items and her heart felt like it was about to explode.

She thanked him and gave him a tip. When he left, she inspected her gifts.

"Whoa, somebody must have someone special in their lives," Christy said as she walked over to Kat's desk.

"Whatever." Kat looked at the card to see who they were from.

In my mind, you are my queen.
I know I hurt you and said you weren't my type, just to be mean,
When in reality, you are the woman of my dreams.
Your beauty is unlike anything I have ever seen.
Your thighs, I love and desire to be in between.
Please give me the chance to show you that I can be your king.
If you will allow me, I know that I can be your everything.

Eric

P.S. I can't wait for tonight.

CHAPTER 14

KAT HELD the card to her heart and looked in Eric's direction. His eyes were on her, taking her in. Watching her expression while reading his poem, he knew he had just scored major points with her. But what he saw when she looked up made the point factor go out the door. Her body language spoke volumes. Her eyes held love and she clutched the card as if it were the most precious thing in this world. He watched as she lovingly stroked each rose. If one didn't know any better, they would assume that she had received the items from the man of her dreams, a man that she loved with all of her heart. That threw Eric for a loop. He knew that she was attracted to him, but he did not know how deep those feelings were. From the way she was looking at him, he would wager that she was just as in love with him as he was with her.

Whoever the mystery guys was, he was going to have to get ready because Eric was playing for keeps. He and Kat were destined to be together. It was time for the extra people to vacate the premises.

As they were leaving work, Kat caught up with him in the parking lot.

"Thank you for the gifts. They are lovely. But you did not have to get me anything."

"You are very welcome. You deserve them and so much more. Yesterday was wonderful. I really enjoy spending time with you and the kids." He was about to say something else, but they were interrupted by Angela.

She walked between the two and looked at Kat. "I see someone has an admirer."

"I guess," Kat said. "Eric sent them to me for helping him out with the proposal."

Eric wondered why she was trying to cover up the real reason for the gift. He noticed how close Angela was to her and a thought occurred to him. No, it couldn't be like that. His Kat couldn't be a lesbian. But the way Angela was acting lately told him otherwise. He got the distinct feeling that she was gearing up for a fight. One starring him.

"Is that right? How nice of you, Eric. It is nice to see you two finally starting to get past your differences. I mean, for a second, I thought I was going to have to transfer one of you. Or maybe even fire one. You guys had so much animosity going on that it was pitiful."

Eric heard her loud and clear. She was intentionally bringing up the past to get Kat to remember the way he had treated her. He hoped like hell Kat wasn't falling for it.

"Well, like you said, it is all in the past." Kat walked over and wrapped her arms around his neck. "Thanks again. I really appreciate the thought." Before she released him, she added, "I'm so looking forward to later on. I can't wait." She smiled as she turned and walked away, leaving both of them staring in her wake.

They watched until she had gotten into her car and pulled off. Angela turned to face Eric. "You do know that I am not about to let you have what's mine, right?" she said, confirming what he already suspected.

"You don't have to let me have anything. If it's yours like you say, then why are you worried?" He was up for the challenge.

"Now that she has someone to make her happy, you want to come in and claim shit. You are the one who broke her in the first place." Angela eyes held fire.

"As I have explained to her, it was a bad time for me. I have made amends and she has accepted my apology. Why are you concerned about it?"

"Like I told you, she is mine, and I'll be damned if I let you hurt her again."

"I am not going to hurt her. That is not even in the equation. I need her in my life."

"You want her. You are curious as to how she feels in bed and that is as far as it goes for you. Admit it. Everyone knows all about you and your inability to commit to one woman. You are a player, a male whore. She deserves so much better than you. So, if I were you, I'd stay away from her. Well, that is if you know what's best for you." She turned and walked to her car.

"Is that a threat?" Eric called out to her.

"Take it however you like," she replied without looking back.

To hell with her and her warning. He jumped in his car and headed home. He was anxious to get ready for a night with Kat.

CHAPTER 15

KAT HAD just stepped into her room from the shower when she heard her doorbell. She glanced at the clock to see if she had lost track of time. Seeing that she still had forty-five minutes before Eric's arrival, she pulled the towel tighter around her and ran to the door to see who it was. Seeing Angela's car in the driveway, she sighed. She did not feel like dealing with her at that particular moment, but she went against her better judgment and opened the door.

"Ummm… Were you waiting for me, baby?" Angela stepped forward and placed a kiss on her neck.

"Angela, not now, I'm expecting someone."

"Who, Eric?"

"Yes, he asked me out and I accepted." She crossed her arms, waiting for Angela to let her know the reason for the visit.

"Aren't you going to invite me in?" Angela pouted.

"I'm sorry, but I really don't have time for a social call. We can hang out tomorrow, if you'd like." Kat didn't want to be mean. She really did like Angela, but she liked Eric a whole lot more. He was the man of her dreams.

"Really, Kat? It's like that with us?"

"We are friends, special friends. I told you that. I also told you that I was not ready for a relationship with you. I enjoy spending time with you and I don't want it to end."

"You want us both, is that it?"

"I am not going to have sex with him anytime soon, if that is what you are worried about. I just want to get to know him, and if it leads to more, then I'm open to the possibilities. I'm not jumping into a relationship with anyone at the moment." She walked towards the stairs to go up to her room, while Angela went to the living room. "I have to finish getting ready. I will be down in a minute."

When she finished dressing, Kat returned to the living room. "What do you think of my dress?" she asked, turning in a circle.

"You look wonderful," Angela said. "He is going to have a hard time trying to keep his hands to himself."

"I am not concerned with that. I trust him to be on his best behavior."

"What if he is expecting more? What will you do then?"

"I am really not getting those kinds of vibes from him. I do not think that he is interested in a booty call with me." She decided not to keep Angela in the dark. She would be upfront and let her know how things progressed.

"I hope, for your sake, that you are right. I would hate to see you all broken up over him again." Angela stood, walked over to Kat, and put a loose strand of hair back in place. "Have fun tonight. You deserve it."

"Thanks for understanding. I really appreciate it." Kat gave Angela a hug and ushered her out the door.

CHAPTER 16

ERIC COULD not believe his eyes when Kat opened the door. He stared, speechless. The woman in front of him had to be the most beautiful woman he had ever had the pleasure of meeting.

"You are making me uncomfortable." Her voice brought him back from his stupor.

"You are beautiful." That was all he could manage to say once he closed his mouth.

"Thank you. You are looking quite dapper yourself."

"Are you ready for our night out?"

"Yes, sir. More than ready." She smiled a smile that made his heart skip a beat. He extended his arm to her and said, "Let's get this show on the road, beautiful lady." She smiled and accepted his arm as they walked out of the door.

Eric was thrilled to finally have his date with Kat. He had envisioned this moment for so long that it seemed surreal. She looked amazing and he would wager that she would taste just as amazing. His mouth watered at the thought of kissing her full, luscious lips. He picked up his napkin and wiped his mouth just in case he had been drooling.

"Do you eat here often?" Her soft voice interrupted his daydream.

"No, I have never been here before, though I have always wanted to try it." He had chosen an Italian restaurant that he had heard good things about. He knew Kat had a thing for Italian food. His mother had told him that.

"So this is a new experience for us both." Kat laughed. "What if we do not like the food?"

Eric winked. "If we do not like it, then I am not paying." He picked up the menu. "But to be fair, this menu is awesome. Everything on here looks delicious."

"It sure does. Too bad I am on a date." She shook her head with a small frown on her face.

"Why is that?" He wondered if she had changed her mind about him.

"Now I have to be all prim and prissy, when I really want to pig out and try a lot of things on this menu."

His head fell back and he roared with laughter at the look of innocence on her face.

"Well, in that case, let's sample, then. And don't try to be all prissy for me, be yourself. We can even share our meals if you'd like." He traced the back of her hand with one finger.

"Okay, that is what I am talking about. I am starving. I was too nervous about tonight to eat today."

He dropped his voice an octave. "So that means that I was on your mind a lot?"

"Yes, you were," she admitted.

"Was it all good?" He continued to play with her hand as he asked questions.

"Yes, very."

"Care to elaborate?" He leaned his head to the side, gauging her reaction.

"No, I don't."

"Why not?"

"I do not think it would be an appropriate topic to discuss at dinner."

He saw desire in her eyes as she spoke and felt a tightening in his pants. Kat did not even know that she was turning him on just by her words alone.

"Is it appropriate for after dinner?" he asked as he took in the way her breasts swelled when she drew in a breath. He wanted to touch them to see if they were as soft as they looked.

"Enjoying the view?" she asked, picking up her wine glass.

"Hell yes." Eric licked his lips. "I have always enjoyed it."

"So this is not the first time that you have taken the liberty to let your eyes wander?"

"Hell no. They wander a lot and very often." His gaze raked over her again.

THE waiter approached the table, breaking the spell. Kat knew that she had to be careful. She had no intention of sleeping with Eric so soon, but if she was not careful, she knew that he could easily convince her otherwise.

The rest of the dinner passed without incident. They had a great time. When they got back to her house, he walked her to the door. She invited him in for coffee, but he declined, saying that it would not be a good idea. His kissed her on the cheek and left after he saw her inside.

That night, her dreams were full of a tall, gorgeous brother with gray eyes exploring her body and the depths of her soul. She woke with wet panties again and told herself to get a handle on her emotions before she did something reckless. Her body craved him. She had never felt this way about any other man before. The feelings that he had awakened in her heart and body were new to her and she was ready to explore them in depth, but she wanted to make sure he wanted the same. She needed him to commit to her and only her; love and desire only her. Maybe one day, she thought as she prepared for her day.

CHAPTER 17

AT WORK, Kat could not stop looking in Eric's direction and she noticed that he was doing the same. If he kept looking at her like that, she knew it would be only a matter of time before she gave him something to think about. She had to break things off with Angela before she took it there, though. She decided to invite her over and tell her that she could not see her anymore. She sent her an IM asking her over for dinner. Angela responded immediately, accepting the offer.

As she prepared dinner, she contemplated how to end things and still be cool with her boss. She was not sure how Angela would react, but it had to be done, and sooner rather than later.

Angela arrived fifteen minutes late for dinner. When Kat opened the door, she began apologizing for being late, blaming it on traffic.

"Don't worry about it," Kat said. She wasn't concerned about tardiness. After all, she was about to break things off.

"How was your day, beautiful?" Angela asked as she leaned in for a kiss. Kat turned her head, letting Angela's lips catch her cheek. She raised an eyebrow. "So, what's up with the dinner?

I thought you wanted to only be friends." She took the glass of wine Kat offered to her.

"We need to talk," Kat told her. Beating around the bush had never really been her thing. She hated it when people did it to her, so she always tried to be upfront.

"And what would you like to talk about, oh beautiful one?" Angela smiled at her.

Kat was uncomfortable with the way the other woman was looking at her. She had a slight smirk on her face. "I really don't think we should see each other outside of the office anymore." The words rushed out in one quick sentence and Kat held her breath.

"Okay."

Kat released the deep breath that she was holding in. "Good, I'm glad that you agree."

"Oh, I don't agree, but I see that he has brainwashed you into thinking that he is really interested in you."

"What?" She was stunned by Angela's words.

"You heard me. You fell for the okeydokey and you know it. He did not want you before, what makes you think that he really wants you now? Nothing has changed. You still look the same. The same shit that he was turned off by before still applies now. You do not dress any different. Your hair is still the same. You have not lost any weight or changed your wardrobe. Think about it, Kat, what is his reasoning for being interested in you now?"

"Oh," was all Kat could get out.

"His only interest is possibly having a threesome with us. That is the only thing that makes sense."

"You don't know that." Kat knew none of what Angela was

saying was true. She had faith in Eric. There was a connection between them, something much stronger than most people knew. When she was with him, she felt complete. Even though she was still a bit confused by the magnitude of her feelings for him, she wasn't going to put a lot of stock in trying to debunk them. She was going to have faith that he would not hurt her and allow him to sweep her off her feet.

"Oh, no? How about we put your little lover boy to the test and see if he passes or fails?"

"What kind of test?"

"Let's invited him to watch me make you cum and give him the option of joining us. Then we will see what is really on his mind. Have you even considered the fact that he might be using you to get to me? I know the guys at work have that bet going on about which one will fuck me first. Maybe he is in on it too. You never know."

Kat thought about what Angela said. Even though she was pissed, there was a throbbing sensation between her legs at the thought of being with both of them. She was not going to admit that to Angela, though. It would be her very own naughty little secret.

After Angela left, Kat fell onto the sofa and wondered about the mess she had gotten herself involved in. She didn't think she could bear seeing Angela and Eric making out. He was meant to be hers and hers alone. She really didn't want to share, even though the idea made her moist.

Needing a distraction, she picked up the remote and flipped through the channels on TV. Nothing really caught her attention, so she turned it off. She walked over to the stereo and put on a rap CD. The fast paced music worked its mojo on her and she felt her body grooving to the beat. She danced around the room while sipping on her wine.

That night, she slept like a log. Her dreams were not plagued with visions of Eric. She woke up the next morning ready to take on the world.

CHAPTER 18

ERIC HAD been watching Kat for most of the day. He knew he should have been focusing on the task at hand. Instead, he sat there gazing in her direction. She had yet to look at him. He knew she was busy with work. Their side was swamped. He looked down at the single file on his own desk. He simply had to finish up the one final project before assuming a new position. A small box of personal items sat on the floor, things he would be taking to his new office on the seventh floor. He was on his way up in the company. He was going to miss being able to see his Kat, but it would all be worth it. Not so much that he needed the money, because he was far from poor, it was the thrill of solving issues and making shit happen.

His computer dinged and he turned his attention to the screen. Angela wanted to meet with him. He wondered what she could possibly have to say to him since she was no longer his boss. They now held the same position in the company, but would be working on a different floor, away from his beautiful Kat, that part sucked about the promotion.

He glanced in Kat's direction and saw that her seat was

empty. He hadn't seen her get up. Standing, he made his way to Angela's office, hoping like hell that she did not take up too much of his lunch hour. She could have waited until after he returned. He figured she just wanted to be a bitch.

Her secretary wasn't at her desk, so he knocked on the door. "Come in," he heard her call.

When he entered, he was surprised to see Kat sitting in one of the chairs. "You wanted to see me?" he asked Angela while his eyes were glued on Kat. She looked luscious to him.

"Yes, have a seat." Angela stood up and walked from behind her desk. She stopped in front of Kat's chair. "I need you to promise that you won't repeat anything that you see or hear in this office, okay?"

He looked at both of the women and wondered what was going on. He shrugged. "Yeah, sure."

"I have seen how you have been watching Kat."

"What does that have to do with anything?" he asked. He looked at Kat. She was looking down at her hands.

Angela placed a hand on Kat's thigh and began caressing it. Eric's eyes followed its every movement. "I know you want her. I can see it in your eyes. Here is the deal: you can have her. But only for this one time and right here in front of me." She leaned forward and kissed Kat on the neck.

Kat glanced over at Eric. She looked torn. His eyes held hers for a minute and then he looked back to Angela. She was kissing her way down to Kat's thighs. He frowned, stroking his goatee. He was disgusted by the entire scene and wondered what type of bullshit they were on.

"Stop!" Kat pushed Angela away.

"Why do you want to stop? You want him and he wants

you. I am giving you permission to explore him just this once."

"Angela, I do not need your permission for anything. I told you that we were through. This is it. It, whatever it was, is over. Please try to understand that." She looked over at Eric. "I am sorry for this. I don't know why I agreed to it. I'm sorry Eric, this is not who I am." She stood and ran out of the office.

Eric stood to make his way out, but then stopped and looked back at Angela. "I am going to suggest that you leave her alone."

She put her hands on her hips and faced him. "Is that right? You can't tell me what the hell to do. She may be a little upset now, but I am sure that I can work it out sooner rather than later."

"Look, I am working on making her my wife, and I will not let you or anyone else get in the way of that. I am in love with her and you just want to toy with her and use her. Stay away Angela, just leave her alone. Don't think you can just prey on her. You were there when I messed up, but all is forgiven now, and you need to step off!"

"Oh, it's like that? Are you trying to threaten me? Do you think you are scaring me? I told you before that you cannot have her and I meant that shit. You think I'm playing, try me."

Eric moved closer to Angela. "I don't give a damn if you are scared or not. What's going on between Kat and I is just that, between me and her. She has told you repeatedly that she does not want to be with you. So, I suggest you take a fucking chill pill."

"You talk a good game, but guess what? She did not say that she wanted your ass either. So, until then, it is all a fair game." She smiled at him with a victorious look in her eyes.

He stood there for a minute before storming out of the office. What Angela said was true. Even though Kat made it a point to let both of them know that she didn't want Angela, she never mentioned wanting him. He had to fix that as soon as possible. He could not allow her to slip away from him this time.

After lunch, he threw himself into his work with a vengeance. Angela floated around the office most of the afternoon. Her Queen Bitch attitude was in full effect. Eric avoided all contact with her. He only had to get through one last afternoon in her presence.

CHAPTER 19

ERIC DID not call before showing up at Kat's house, wanting to catch her off guard. He was not impressed with by the display in Angela's office and needed to find out where they stood. It was time-out for that bullshit with Angela.

Kat's car was in the driveway as he pulled up. He strolled up to the door, trying to think of a good reason for him stopping by. As he got closer, he heard noises coming from the back-yard. He made a detour and headed toward the sounds. In the back, he saw Kat moving around in the yard. It looked like she was getting ready to work in her garden. He stood there for a second, just taking her in.

"Hi there," he finally called out to her.

Kat whirled around. "Eric," she said shaking a finger at him. He saw a hint of a smile before it disappeared. "You're going to get enough of sneaking up on me like that."

"I am sorry. I did not mean to startle you. I just wanted to check on you to see if you were okay." He walked over to where she stood.

"I'm straight. Thanks for being concerned."

"Hey, that is what friends do, right?" He let his eyes caress hers for a moment. He could tell that she was feeling him too. Instead of making a move, he offered to help her with the gardening.

"That's okay. I got this. I don't want to be the reason you get your new suit dirty. I know y'all pretty boys hate getting dirty," she teased.

He took the bag of fertilizer from her hand. "Oh, so now I am a pretty boy? I will take that. Any compliment from you is special." He smiled at her before walking over to the flowers she had set out to be planted and kneeling next to them.

"I'm just saying I don't want you to have to schedule an emergency manicure because you have dirt caked underneath your nails." She got down on the ground beside him.

"We can avoid all of that if you give me one after we're done."

Kat gave him a blank look. "Give you what?"

"A manicure. You can give me one after we are done. That way, I won't have to try and find an open nail shop. You would be saving me a lot of time and energy." He grinned.

"Hmmm… Well, I guess that is the least I can do. I mean, you are helping me, so I should repay you some way."

"I can think of plenty of ways that you can repay me, but I will settle for the manicure for now." He let his eyes roam over her body so that she would know exactly what he meant.

THEY worked for a while with her telling him about each of the flowers they planted. He was amazed at the way she cared for each one of them. She told him of her plans to have her own little slice of heaven right in her back yard. She said that she wanted to be able to sit out at her table, sipping a glass of wine and enjoying the sweet smell of her flowers. He could envision her doing just that. But in his mind, he was sitting at that table with her, sharing the bottle of wine.

When it started getting dark, Kat suggested they call it a day. After they put the gardening items away, she invited Eric in to clean up while she put on a quick supper.

"I guess I will be heading home," he said as he walked out of the bathroom.

"Are you sure? I thought you wanted your manicure?"

"It's cool. You can give it to me another time." He wanted to stay. He needed her to ask him to stay. He walked toward the door.

"You might as well stay and have dinner with me. I put enough on for the both of us," Kat said.

"Oh, did you?"

"Yes, I figured that was the least I could do for all of the help. We got a lot done, and I probably wouldn't have gotten half of it complete if it wasn't for you. So, come on back in here and let me feed you and then I'll give you your manicure as promised." She grabbed his hand and pulled him in the kitchen.

Mission accomplished, he thought with a smile.

As promised, she gave him a manicure while they waited on dinner. There were plenty of moments when he had to fight the urge to pull her in his arms and devour her sweet-looking lips, but he resisted each time. He could sense her need for him also, but he knew the timing was not right. He had to make sure he was the only person on her mind and that she was completely done with Angela.

"So, what is up with you and Angela?" he asked as they sat down to dinner.

"Nothing much. I was lonely and she comforted me." She looked down, her cheeks red.

"Are you guys and item? Or were you?"

"I was thinking about it, but I could not wrap my mind around being in a lesbian relationship."

"Do you have feelings for her?" He needed to know what he was up against.

"I like her, she is cool. We had fun together, but then she started being possessive and showing traits of jealousy, which was not okay with me." She looked at him. He knew she was checking for his reaction, so he kept his face void of any emotions.

"Who was she jealous of? I have not seen you with many people, nor do I see you hanging out a lot." He took a big bite of his food and waited for her to answer.

She looked down at her plate then back up at him. "She is jealous of you. She thinks that we have something going on."

"Is that right? What does she think is going on between us?" He already knew, but he wanted her take on it. He wanted to see where her mind was.

"I do not know. I guess she thinks we are intimate. Or that you only want to sleep with me. It is all crazy to me." She laughed, but he could tell that she was nervous.

"Why do you think it is crazy?"

"Because we are not doing anything. I am an honest person. If I say something, then that is how it is. No more, no less. She thinks that I am weak and that I can be persuaded to do things against my will. That shit is hilarious to me." She laughed again as she took a sip of her wine.

Eric raised an eyebrow. "Maybe she sees something that you are not seeing."

"Naw, it is nothing like that. Do not let my demeanor fool you. I notice a lot of things. And if I don't want something, then there is not a damn thing anyone can do to convince me otherwise." Her look told him that she meant every word that she spoke.

"Well, you must know that I am very attracted to you and that I have been for a while. I am interested in seeing where things can go with us." It was time up for the games.

"Yes, I know that. And I also know that Angela has been trying to throw shade. I know all of this."

"How do you feel about it, about me?"

"I think the path we are taking is the best one. If it is meant to be, then no one can get in the way of it. I am very interested in you too. So interested that I need to take this one slow. I want it to last if we are meant, so I don't want to rush. You are special to me Eric."

Relief spread throughout his body. He reached across the table and took her hand in his. "So you are fine with us being friends, not rushing into anything, but simply letting nature take its course?"

"Yes, I am okay with that. I prefer it. It gives us a chance to really get to know one another." She squeezed his hand.

"Sometimes, it is hard as hell for me to resist you. At times, I want to rip your clothes off and make love to you right on the spot." His eyes held hers. His desire was strong. He could see himself taking her right there on the table. "Today, in Angela's office, I saw a look of lust on your face. Did you want that to happen?"

"Um… Why do you ask?" she stammered.

"If you want that, then just let me know."

"But you were upset by it," she said.

"I was not upset by you wanting that. I was pissed off at the fact that someone else was touching you. I want to be the only one to touch you, to please you. If you want that after we get to where we need to be, then it will be fine. But not with Angela, never with her." Resisting the temptation to pull her close to him, he stood and took his dishes to the sink.

"I can do that. And why not with her?" Kat asked.

"Because of your past with her and the fact that she wants you." He shook his head. "Nope, I cannot have that. She is like Public Enemy Number One for me." He turned to face her. "Look, I think it is best if I leave, because it is hard as hell for me to contain myself."

"Okay." Kat stood. "Well, thanks for helping me with the garden." She smiled at him as she began loading the dishwasher.

Eric watched her for a moment, all kinds of inappropriate thoughts running through his mind. He took a deep breath. "Yeah, I am about to head out. Come and walk me to the door."

She followed to the front door. There, he turned to her and pulled her to him in a tight embrace.

"One day, you will be all mine, sweet, beautiful Kat," he whispered, his lips grazing her ear. He turned and walked to his car without looking back. He knew that if he did, he would go back and take what she would willingly offer to him.

KAT stood rooted in the same spot until Eric pulled off. Then she closed the door and headed for a cold shower. What the hell did Angela know? He did not want to share. He was not interested in a threesome and he was jealous. She smiled to herself. One day soon, she will have him and not just in her dreams. One day very soon indeed.

CHAPTER 20

IN THE weeks that passed, Kat and Eric grew closer. They sometimes had lunch together in Eric's new office. He had even asked her to help him decorate it. She was ecstatic to have her influence in his office. She kept it simple and modern. His favorite color was blue. So most of the things she chose were blue and grey. He said that he loved what she had done to his space and he did not change one single thing, he only added to the décor and that was a picture of them together in her back-yard out by her Koi pond. Angela tried to schedule meetings or assign Kat tasks so they would not be able to spend time together, but Eric would take his lunch at whatever time Kat took hers.

Eric knew that one of the reasons he got the new position was because of Angela trying to keep them apart. He and a few other people had applied for the job. The one person they all felt was going to get the job was beat out by him. That was okay with him because his salary had increased tremendously. Kat would definitely be able to be a housewife if that is what she desired. They could look for a new house or he could move in with her. Whatever she wanted to do was fine with him. He had a feeling that she would want him to move in and they would keep her house. She was in love with it, and to be honest, he felt at home there himself.

The two spent hours on the phone after work. Eric was working his plan and taking his time in getting to know Kat. The more he found out, the more he knew that she was the one, the woman he would spend the rest of his life with. He loved the way she laughed and he adored her free spirit. When they were together, they simply enjoyed one another's company. There was no drama and hardly any negative conversation. He felt completely at ease with her. Finally, he was happy. He had a reason for waking up in the morning and a reason to smile. He felt so alive, and he owed it all to her. His beautiful Kat.

They did not go out on any more dates and that was okay with the both of them. Eric knew that Kat was busy getting her house in order, but he could not seem to stay away from her. He would often pop up and spend time helping her with odd jobs and she would repay him by inviting him to stay for dinner. Each time he left her house, he had to go straight home and take a cold shower. His resolve was growing weaker by the day. He decided that he would continue offering his services to her until the time was right for them to become one.

He admired her dedication to getting her house the way she wanted it. He could see the light in her eyes when she told him about a new project that she had taken on. He adored her and he wanted to be right there with her.

One day, after helping her plant some trees out back, they had a picnic in the backyard. When they finished eating, they lay out on a blanket and looked at the clouds, confiding in one another about their wants, fears, and desires. Conversation came easily between the two. Kat smelled of pears and her skin was glowing. All day, he had fought the urge to kiss her. The low neckline on her sundress granted him a nice view of the swell of her breasts and he could feel his restraint weakening. He wanted to make love to her on the blanket they lay on, but the timing still wasn't quite right.

When her mother stopped by, he was relieved by the interruption. He left the two women and went to the gym to relieve some stress. He figured that he was bound to be in the best shape of his life as much as Kat had him working out.

Later that night, he called her. She had called him while he was at the gym and he was just now getting around to calling her back.

"Hey, beautiful," he said when she answered.

"Hi, Eric," she purred. He could tell that she was genuinely happy to hear from him.

"I am sorry that it took so long to get back to you."

"It is okay as long as you did get back to me."

"What are you over there doing?"

"If you would have stayed, then you would know what I am doing."

"If I would have stayed, I would probably be doing you right at this very moment."

"Maybe that would not have been such a bad idea. In fact, I think I might have enjoyed it very much."

"Soon, my beautiful Kat, very soon, I will make you mine. You do know that once we go there, there will be no turning back, right? I am playing for keeps. I am not interested in a fling. I am ready for more. I am ready for my wife." His mind was made up. He was ready to claim her for his.

"Neither am I interested in a fling. I want so much more."

"What do you want, love?" The last word slipped out. "I mean, Kat."

Kat was quiet for a minute. "I want you."

Eric groaned. "I had to do everything within my power not to rip that dress off of you and take you right there in the back yard on that blanket. You smelled so sweet and I could imagine you tasting the same way. Tell me, my beautiful Kat, do you taste as sweet as you smell?"

"Why don't you find out for yourself?"

"Oh, I plan to do just that and so much more, sexy lady. I hope that you are ready for me, baby, because once I get you, I am putting it down for real. I need to have you only wanting me."

CHAPTER 21

ON HIS way to the gym, Eric passed Kat's house. He saw her outside trying to move something heavy inside, so he turned around and went back to help. She was so busy that she didn't even hear him approach.

"You know you could have called me to help you," he said.

Startled, she dropped the end of the furniture she was holding. "Eric, you scared the hell out of me," she exclaimed while clutching her chest. "Why do you keep doing that?"

He laughed at her reaction.

"Why are you trying to move this big thing by yourself anyways?" He examined the piece, trying to decide on the best way to get it in her house.

"I just wanted to get it done. You know people want to charge an arm and a leg for helping these days." She sat down on the step.

"Kat, I told you that I am here for you. You can call on me at times like this. It is what friends are for, remember?"

"That is sweet of you, but you really don't have to help me. I see that you were on your way to the gym. I don't want to be a bother."

"Whatever. What all are you trying to move in?" He noticed a U-Haul backed up in the yard. He walked over and took a look in the back. "You were planning on putting all of this in the house by yourself?"

"Yes. I mean, I would have eventually gotten it all in there."

"Yeah, okay. And probably would have strained something in the process." He walked over to his car and took out his phone. He made a few calls before joining her on the step. "I called a few guys to come over here and get it done for you."

"Really? Wow, thanks." She smiled.

"I told you it is no problem."

Her smile faded. "Wait. How much are they going to charge?"

"It's all good. We got this. You just let us know where you want everything and it will be a wrap."

"I can't just let you guys do all of that work without some sort of payment." She looked thoughtful. "How about dinner? I can fix you guys some victuals for the help?"

"Now that right there sounds like a winner. I'm always ready for a good ole' home-cooked meal." He rubbed his stomach.

Kat laughed. "Didn't you eat anything today?"

"Yeah, but it was much earlier. I was going to grab something on the way home from the gym. You know I'm not much of a cook. Now, barbecue is my thing. That, I can do very well."

"When is the last time you grilled?"

"It has been a while. You know work has been having us strung out. All I be wanting to do on the weekend is chill."

"How about if I run to the store and get the stuff for a barbecue?"

"Hey, that is a great idea. Yeah, that's perfect."

They made a list out of things to get from the store and Kat showed him where the grill and charcoal were. While he got started with lighting it, she ran inside and grabbed her purse to head out to the store.

WHEN Kat got back, she saw three other cars at her house. She got out and the men walked over to her car. They all spoke and got the bags from the car. Two of them she knew from work. The other guy she had never seen before.

"Kat, this is my best friend, Tim. Tim, this is Kat."

Tim took her hand and gave it a kiss. "Ahhh... finally I get to meet the beautiful Kat."

Eric pushed him playfully. "Enough of that. Let's get this truck cleared off so we can get to the food."

"We can do the truck," Tim said. "You need to go ahead and get on that grill. We got this. You handle up on that."

"Aight, cool, I can do that."

Tim and the other two guys started unloading the truck while Kat seasoned the meat and Eric threw it on the grill. While it cooked, she made potato salad and baked beans to go with their dinner.

After all of the furniture was in its proper place and the food was ready, they all sat out on the back deck throwing down and talking. Eric made it a point to sit next to Kat.

"So, Kat, when are you going to paint your library?" Tim asked her. She had shown the guys each room and told them how she planned to decorate it.

"I am thinking of doing it next weekend. That is, if Angela

doesn't work us like slaves this week." They all agreed with her on that.

"I already told you that I can help you with all of this," Eric reminded her. "You can get it done much faster with more hands. Then you will have more time to play. And besides, I think you should put in a transfer to my department so I can keep an eye on you." He winked at her.

"I don't want to take advantage of your help. And you know Angela is not going to sign off on a transfer. It would be too much like right. Her mission is to keep me miserable."

He leaned over so that only she could hear him. "You aren't taking advantage of me. I want to help you with all of this. I told you that I love spending time with you. You are mine. So she might as well get used to it."

CHAPTER 22

AFTER A couple of hours, Eric's friends left. Kat sent plates home with all of them. Eric returned to the kitchen after seeing Tim off. He propped up against the door frame and watched her move around the kitchen.

"Why are you looking at me like that?"

"No reason in particular," he said without batting an eye.

"Are you just going to stand there and watch or would you like something to drink?" She had begun to feel a little nervous. True, they had been out to dinner and were developing a great relationship, but at that moment, she felt that his look screamed anything but "Let's continue being friends." His look said that tonight was the night that they took their relationship to a different level, and she was scared. It had been a minute since she had been with a man and she was slightly worried about pleasing him thoroughly.

"I think I am going to stand here and watch."

"Okay, do what you do," she conceded.

"You don't want me to do that."

"Why?" She knew she should not have taken the bait. She

could not help it, though. She knew beyond a shadow of a doubt that tonight was going to change everything between them.

"You aren't ready for that."

"How do you know?" she challenged.

"I just know." He had not moved an inch and his eyes still remained on her.

"What am I not ready for, Eric?"

He took slow deliberate steps towards her. Once in front of her, he looked into her eyes before leaning down to capture her lips. At first, it was a simple sweet kiss, but then it grew deeper and deeper until Kat was sure that she was going to pass out from sheer pleasure.

"Damn, Kat, baby, you taste so delicious," Eric said against her mouth. He didn't give her time to respond. He wrapped his arms around her and pulled her in closer to him.

Kat went willingly, no hesitation. She let her hands go up around his neck and pulled his head closer to her so that she could feast on his mouth. His taste was divine, unlike anything she had ever tasted.

The phone ringing brought them back to earth. Kat realized that it was her phone and raced over to answer it. "Hello," she said breathlessly.

"What are you over there doing?" her sister asked.

"Minding my business. Why?" She turned towards Eric. He was leaning against the counter, looking at her. Her eyes trailed down his body and stopped right below his waist. He was excited. His dick was hard and she could see the print. It looked enormous. He smiled at her and she momentarily forgot that her sister was on the phone.

"Um, excuse me, did you hear what I just said?" Her sister broke her concentration again.

"What did you say? I'm sorry, something had caught my attention." He was walking over to her. Her heart started beating faster.

"I said that I was calling to see if you could keep the kids for me tonight? I have a hot date and I'm not trying to miss it. Honey, he got bank and a big dick to match." Her sister went on and on while her attention was on Eric's approach. Then his lips as they came closer to hers. He took his kiss while she was still holding the phone.

"Hey, girl, can you do it for me?"

"Umm, I'm sorry, I can't," she stuttered as Eric began to kiss her neck.

"Why not? Please, girl? I know I always ask you to keep them, but this time, this might be the man of my dreams."

"Man of your dreams?" Kat asked.

Eric took the phone from her and spoke into it. "I'm sorry, but Kat is kind of busy right now with the man of her dreams." He hung up the phone.

"You are the man of my dreams?" she asked.

"I don't know. You tell me."

"No, I think not. I think I will keep it to myself."

"And how long do you think you will be able to do that, my beautiful Kat?" He pulled her to him continued feasting on her neck.

"Hmmm... I .... Oh, Eric," she moaned.

"Yes, baby?"

"I want to feel you inside of me," she finally admitted to him.

"Oh, baby, how I want to be inside of you too."

"Come upstairs." Kat told him.

Eric took the lead and headed up the stairs. He stopped suddenly, causing her to wonder if he had changed his mind. He leaned back against the wall and looked at her. His eyes held so much desire that she was taken aback.

"I love looking at you," he said. She could hear her own heart beating in her ears. At the rate it was going, she was bound to have a heart attack before they even had intercourse.

"That's nice to know." She was at a loss for words. Her dream man was informing her that he had wanted her more than she had ever known. It was she whom he wanted.

He beckoned her to him. She made her way to him slowly. Once she was standing directly in front of him, she began to undress him. His shirt was the first thing to go. Kat took her time in adoring his well-defined chest. She knew he was beautiful, but she had no idea to what extreme. She lowered herself to the steps in front of him and let her fingers slide up his legs until she reached the object of her many fantasies. Next his sweats and then his boxers were gone. She could not take her eyes off it. Her fingers found their way to his member and traced the throbbing veins.

"Kat." His voice was hoarse.

Eric's mind was in a Kat-induced fog. All that he could think about was the way her hands felt on him. With the way she was touching him, he knew he would not be able to last long. He let his head fall back as her hand enclosed his hardness. Then he felt something wet flicker across it. He looked down just in time to see himself disappear in her mouth. A sharp intake of breath was all that he could manage. Her mouth was warm and wet. Oh so very wet.

He tried to think of something to maintain his composure, but she wouldn't let him. He felt her hands close around him as she continued on her mission to get him excited. She released his shaft and got into position to take him inside of her mouth. All that could be heard were her slurps, and that was driving him further toward edge. He gripped the back of her head and gave in to the urge to bury himself deep down her throat. The further he pushed, the more she accepted. He knew he was done for. He couldn't take the sweet torture that she was inflicting on his body. He felt it growing in the pit of his stomach. "I'm gonna cum," he growled, warning her, letting her know that she should probably move before it was too late. Instead, she took him deeper into her mouth and let him release there without once stopping.

Eric's mind was blank. What he had just experienced was beyond anything he'd ever had done to him before. He'd had his share of women and he was no stranger to oral sex, but with Kat, it took on a whole new meaning.

His heart finally returned to the normal speed. They stood looking at one another before he brought his mouth down to hers. He tasted himself on her tongue. That only gave him another erection. Kat was doing something to his body and he hoped that he was ready for it all. He wanted to make sure that he gave as well as he got.

She took his hand and pulled him to her bedroom. It was his turn to have his way with her and he was ready. He let his fingers linger on her arms before he drew her in for another sample of her sweet lips. He was never big on kissing, but her lips called out to him. They looked like they were made for kissing, and preferably by him. His let his kisses trail from her mouth to her neck.

He felt her trembling in his arms as he placed delicate kisses on her neck and knew that he had found his treasure. Once in her bedroom, she opened wide for him. He applied more pressure then began to sucking harder in that spot. He heard her moan a little. He backed her up to the bed and gently pushed her down before climbing on the bed with her. Her pupils were dilated and her breathing was shallow. He knew it wasn't going to take long to get her to where he wanted her to be. He started at her feet and kissed his way up to her lips. He gave her a gentle bite before deepening the kiss. Kat opened up again and gave him all that he craved.

"So sweet," he moaned as he kissed her. He retraced his path and made his way to her ample breasts. Her nipples were hard and ready for him to sample. He took his time in giving each one his undivided attention before making his way to her stomach. He thought that her skin was so soft and smelled so sweet. As his lips grazed the top of her thigh, he guided her legs open even wider. He closed his eyes and breathed her in before leaning down and introducing her to his skillful tongue, hoping he was better than any before him. Over and over, he let his tongue please her. He held on to her hips as he made her cum repeatedly. Even when she tried to run, he held on and continued with his quest.

When he finally felt like she had had enough, he released her clit from his suction and looked up at her. She looked exhausted. He figured she was too tired to go on and on like he really wanted.

"Are you okay, baby?" he asked.

"Yes, I am fine." She answered with her eyes still closed.

Rising, he rolled a condom on and slid into her wetness. He felt her walls constrict almost immediately. She clung to him and began calling his name.

His front was drenched from her orgasm. He was so turned on he couldn't think straight. He pumped furiously and felt his nut coming. It started out as a seed in his stomach and grew into a full-blown beast. He roared as his semen filled the condom. For a second, he wished that he hadn't worn one. He wanted his seed to be inside of her, but did not tell her that for fear of running her off.

He still had not gone down or removed himself from her body. He needed more of her and planned on getting all she was willing to give. Just as he let his lips close around one of her nipples, his phone rang. He was content with letting it go to voicemail, but it kept ringing.

CHAPTER 23

"YOU BETTER get that," Kat told him. "It might be important."

"Yeah," he said. He made his way to the stairs to get his phone. When he picked it up, he saw that it was Tim.

"You better have a damn good reason for interrupting me," he said as soon as he answered.

"Eric, man, I ... I had an accident and I'm trapped in the car."

Eric felt a cold chill go down his spine. "Are you hurt badly? Did you call the police? Where are you?"

"I ... uh ... not too far from my house." Tim's voice was low and kind of hard to hear. "Call 911. I'm trapped and I can't dial."

Eric called Kat and told her to dial 911. She ran for her phone, dialed the number and he continued to talk to Tim.

"Man, I'm on my way, just keep talking to me brother," he said, trying to keep his friend's mind occupied. Kat put the phone on speaker to stay on with the 911 operator and she and Eric quickly dressed. They got into Eric's car and sped to Tim's location.

Once they arrived on the scene, Eric was terrified. Tim's car was wrapped around a tree and he saw his friend's head lying to the side. He approached the car and Tim told him that he press the button on the wheel and said Eric. Eric wondered why he didn't say 911, but that wasn't at all important. At a time Eric and his friends used to dog Tim for having so many gadgets in his car, but he was secretly thanking God that he had that feature, because from the looks of it, Tim could not have reached for his phone.

KAT stood by Eric with her arm around his waist, and when they took Tim to the hospital, she was right there with him. They sat together waiting for word from the doctor. When Tim's family started to arrive, she faded into the background, not really talking to anyone. They were all focused on Tim and wondering if he was going to pull through.

Seeing Eric with his head down, she placed her hand on his back to offer him comfort. She felt bad for him, knowing that this had to be hard on him. He had lost his mother not too long ago and Tim was the closest friend. He looked back at her for a moment without saying anything.

"Would you like for me to get you some coffee or something?" she asked.

"Yeah, coffee would be great," he told her.

When she returned, she saw that more of Tim's family had arrived and they were looking at her when she entered the waiting room and sat down next to Eric. He seemed to be in his own little world until she handed him his cup of coffee.

"Thanks, Kat," he said. His voice was so low that she barely heard him.

"No problem."

After a few minutes, her hand returned to its place on his back. For the next twenty minutes or so, they sat there like that, him drinking his coffee and her rubbing his back, trying to comfort him as best she could.

THE doctor finally came out and told them Tim was out of the woods, but he was still unconscious.

Eric asked Kat if she wanted to grab a bite while they waited and she said yes. As they walked to the cafeteria, he asked her over and over if she wanted him to take her home. She insisted that she was fine and told him that she would stay with him.

Even though he did not tell her, he was delighted that she chose to stay. Her being there with him was such a comfort. He adored her so much. He'd thought that he loved her before, but now he was completely sure of it. This was the woman for him, the one that God had put on this earth specifically for him.

"Why are you looking at me like that?" She had noticed that he kept throwing glances her way.

"No reason. How is your sandwich?" He asked her.

"It's fine. I just wished that it had onions on it." She laughed. Kat loved onions on just about everything. Being that she was used to being by herself, she often indulged in putting them on her sandwiches. Tonight, however, she took them off to avoid the dreaded onion breath.

"Oh whatever. You took them off remember?"

"I know, but I couldn't be all around people with onion breath." She tilted her head to the side and looked innocent.

He smiled at her. "See, we both could have had onion breath. I would have been cool with that. But when you took yours off, I followed suit. Damn, woman, you had me getting rid of my onions for nothing. I should spank you for that."

"And why did you do that if you wanted them? Maybe you should spank me." She batted her eyes at him, having an idea what he was going to say. Still she wanted to hear it from his mouth.

"Because I can't be having onion breath if I am planning on collecting some more of those oh-so-sweet kisses of yours. And you are definitely going to get it now."

"How many kisses do you plan on getting?" She felt her pulse quickening.

"As many as I can get with the time I have left."

"What about the spanking? How many swats am I in for?" Kat ran her fingers through her hair as she thought back to the way his hands felt on her body. She knew she was blushing, but that's the affect he had on her.

"Hmmm… I'm not sure as of yet. We should wait and see before I decide on a set amount. You know, just in case you act out again." He bit his lip and his gaze raked over her body.

"Why are you looking at me like that?" Her nerves were all over the place and her body was still reeling from the aftermath of their lovemaking.

She wanted more; her body wanted a lot more. The situation wasn't ideal at the moment, though, and she felt a twinge of guilt for thinking about sexing him up while they were here at the hospital to see if Tim was okay.

ERIC convinced Kat to go for a walk with him outside in the park near the hospital. They walked hand-in-hand for a while then went back. Before going inside, he led her to the side of the building, out of the public view.

"Time to pay up, baby," he told her as his head dipped down. He brushed his lips across hers before settling in to a toe-curling one that made her feel faint. She wanted to lift her foot like women did in movies after experiencing The Kiss.

"Thanks for being here with me, Kat. You have no idea how much this really means to me."

"I will always be here for you. That's what friends are for, remember?" Kat told him jokingly. In reality, there was no other place that she'd rather be.

"I don't want to be just friends anymore," he said.

"What would you like for us to be?" She hoped that he wanted her just as much as she wanted him.

"Whatever you like, Kat, just as long as I'm able to be with you, kiss you, make love to you." He traced the outline of her lower lip with his finger.

She knew that he was waiting for her to say something when his phone chimed. Saved by the bell, she thought.

"They said Tim just woke up," Eric said after he got off the phone. "Let's go see how he is." He took her hand again and made their way back into the hospital.

CHAPTER 24

BACK IN the waiting room, all eyes were on Eric and Kat when they walked in. He did not release her hand until it was time for him to go back and see his friend. As soon as he was out of hearing range, Tim's mother walked over to Kat.

"Why are you here?" she asked..

Kat frowned. "I came with Eric."

"I can see that. What I meant was why are you here? This is family business." She turned and walked away.

The woman wanted her gone, but that was too damn bad. She was going to stay there with Eric until he told her that he wanted her to leave. She didn't know what the woman's problem was. Whatever it was, she would have to deal with it because she couldn't make her leave.

After what seemed like an eternity with the Tim's family gawking at her, Eric came back to the waiting area.

Tim's mom jumped up and gave him a big hug. They talked for a few minutes before he walked over to Kat.

"Are you ready to go?"

"I'm ready whenever you are," she told him.

"Well, Mama Bee, I'm about to head out. Kat and I both have to be at work early in the morning."

"Did you say Kat?" she asked.

"Yes, ma'am, this is Katlynn Jones. I'm sorry, I thought that I introduced everyone." He turned to Kat and introduced her to Mama Bee told her the names of the other people in the room.

"Honey child, why didn't you tell me that you were Kat?" Mama Bee asked. "Lawdy, I'm up here giving you a hard time because I'm thinking all the while that you were just some random hoochie."

Eric laughed out loud. "Why would you think that, Mama Bee? You know you be doing too much on a daily basis."

"Boy, I told your momma that I was going to look out for you, and that is what I was doing." She turned to Kat, "I have wanted to meet you for some time now. Donna spoke so highly of you that I feel as if I know you too."

"She was a wonderful woman," Kat said, stealing a glance at Eric.

Mama Bee caught on to Kat's expression and told her, "He's fine. His mom was my best friend in the whole wide world. I'm also his godmother. That is how I know of you. She told me about the picnic and all." She took Kat's hand. "She adored you."

"I'm sorry it was under these conditions that you two met," Eric said. "The next time will be under better circumstances. But we have to go so that we can rest up for tomorrow. Kat's boss is hell on wheels and she has been itching to fire her for the slightest reason."

"And if she does, you need to let me know and I will catch her after work and whoop the shit out of her ass," Tim's mother said as she gave Eric a hug. Then she turned to Kat and enveloped her in her arms, telling her that they should get together for lunch sometimes.

Kat agreed and waved to everyone as Eric led her from the hospital. In the car, she turned to him and said, "Tim's family seems nice."

"Yeah, they are great folks. Sometimes they can be a little loud, but they are still wonderful." He chuckled.

"They seem to care about you a whole lot."

"Like she said, I have known her my whole life. She has always been like a second mom to me. If I wasn't home, I was at their house. The same was true for Tim. We grew up like brothers."

She heard the love in his voice for his extended family. It was good to know that he was not totally alone as she once suspected he was. He still had people who cared for him as a family should.

"That's nice. They all seem sweet. Well, not at first." She laughed at how they had sized her up.

Eric glanced at her. "What do you mean?"

She looked out the window at the buildings as they cruised through the city. "Oh, they had me on the hot spot for a while."

"No shit? What did they say?"

"They were wondering why was I there with you. Basically, they were trying to find out if I was some trick."

"My bad, I didn't mean to leave you in there with them interrogating you." He looked over at her again.

"It's straight. I survived it." She patted his thigh.

He looked over at her and licked his lips. He took one hand off the steering wheel and placed it on her thigh. He caressed her all the way to her house. When they got there, he got out and opened the door for her. She asked him if he wanted to come in for coffee and he said no, it was already late and they both needed to be at work early the next day.

He gave her a quick peck before heading home.

CHAPTER 25

KAT GRABBED her phone to read her message. She figured it was from Eric, because she had made him promise to call her when he arrived home.

As expected, it was him. In her reply, she asked him why he didn't call her. He said that he just wanted to send a quick message before climbing in the shower. She understood that, but she wanted to hear his voice.

She dialed his number. The phone rang three times before he answered. "Why are you calling me?"

She paused. "I'm sorry." she snapped. "I didn't know that I could not call you."

"You can call whenever you like. You know that. But there is a specific reason why I did not call you tonight."

"And what is that reason?"

"Your voice, that's the reason. I did not want to hear your sexy-ass voice. I miss you as it is and hearing your voice only makes it worse.

"Oh." Her heart skipped at his words.

"I know that we both need to rest up for work in the

morning, but damn, I want to be so deep up in you right now that it hurts." His admission was her undoing. She felt her panties becoming damp.

"Now, I see what you mean. Sorry I called." Her thoughts flew back to earlier and the things he had done to her body. She wanted more.

"Yeah, you shouldn't have. But check this, I'm about to get off this phone for now. I'll send you a text in a little bit." He hurried off the phone.

Kat jumped in the shower and took her time scrubbing her body with her new Victoria's Secret body wash. It was Eric's favorite. He had told her on plenty of occasions.

Just as she was about to climb in bed her doorbell rang.

"Who in the hell is it at this time of the night?" she asked herself while heading to the door. She hoped it wasn't Angela.

She looked out the window and saw Eric's car. Her heart sped up and she raced to the door and swung it open. Eric stood at the door with a huge grin on his handsome face.

"Why didn't you tell me you were coming back?" Kat asked as she jumped into his arms.

"I wanted to surprise you, baby." He put his head to hers. "Damn, Kat, you smell so edible. I'm just in time for dessert, I see."

Her skin tingled in anticipation of his kisses. She was definitely ready for his loving. She needed more of it. She had become addicted in a matter of hours. Now, she couldn't even fathom being without him. She pulled him in the house and drew him in her arms. She raised her head and let her tongue trace his bottom lip before biting it lightly.

He grabbed her chin and deepened their kiss. "I know I

said that we needed to rest up for tomorrow, but I need you so much more. I need to make love to you, Kat. I need to hear you calling my name. I need to feel your legs around me and your mouth on me." He lowered his mouth to her neck and inhaled deeply.

"Eric, you are driving me wild." Kat moaned as she felt him marking his territory. He embraced and held her tightly and all of her defenses fell. She had no more reserves, no more mountains that needed to be moved. She was ready, completely ready, to love Eric like he deserved to be loved.

He moaned into her mouth. "Can I stay the night, Kat?"

"Yes, you can." Her eyes rolled back in her head as she felt a hand come up and cup one of her breasts. He let his thumb graze her nipple as he sucked her bottom lip. His other hand took hold of her behind and gave it a gentle squeeze. "Eric, I need to feel you inside of me."

"Not yet, baby."

"Please?" she begged. The fire between her legs was intensified.

She pushed him to the couch and he fell back onto it. He looked up at her with shock on his face. She opened her legs and began gyrating her hips for him. His eyes were glued to her lower body. She turned her back to him so that he could take in the rear view.

After a few minutes of dancing, she stood with her legs apart, her back still to him. Slowly, she eased her panties down and stepped out of them. She threw them to the side and looked at him through her open legs. His breathing was erratic and she could see him at full attention.

"Come here, Kat," he ordered.

Instead of complying, she turned around and lowered herself to the floor. Then she crawled over to him and took him into her mouth.

Kat took her time in loving him. She wanted to make sure he felt every emotion, everything in her heart, as she brought him to his peak. Over and over, she licked and sucked until he stiffened even harder. Then she stood up and climbed onto his lap.

The look in his eyes told her everything that she needed to know. He made her feel loved with that one look.

"I'm in love with you, Eric," she admitted, not quite sure if it was too soon to be saying it, but going on her gut instincts.

"I'm in love with you too, Kat. I need you in my life, baby." His mouth claimed hers as their tongues slow danced together. His hands roamed over her delicate skin. She felt his hand slide between them as he guided himself to her opening.

"I don't want to use protection," he whispered to her. "I want to have babies with you, a lot of babies."

"Are you sure that's what you want?" She wanted that too. She wanted a family with this man. She wanted to be with him forever. She was ready to take a chance on love again.

"Yes, I am positive. I have always been sure of us," he said as he pulled her down on his hard shaft.

She held her breath as she was lowered all the way down to the base, with him filling her completely. She released the air in her chest from the sensation he gave her. He was long and thick and she was very tight. It had been a very long time since she'd had sex with a man and the one time earlier was not enough for her to become fully accustomed to his girth.

"Oh, Eric," she wailed as he let his tongue trace the outline of her ear while moving his hips ever so slightly.

"You feel so good wrapped around me. I could stay like this forever," he whispered in her ear. Then he began marking his territory all over again. She felt him latching on to some already sensitive spots.

"What are you doing?" she asked him as she grinded her hips to the beat of the music.

"Letting these other mofos know that you are taken," he mumbled into her neck.

"Am I, Eric?" The rhythm of her hips had picked up. She was comfortable with his size now.

"OOOOOh yes. Damn, Kat, yes."

Kat leaned into him and clamped onto his neck to return the favor as she did her best to take him on the ride of his life.

No more words were spoken as they held on to one another for dear life. They made love all night and early into the morning, both not wanting it to end.

CHAPTER 26

IN KAT'S dream, Eric's head was buried between her legs and his mouth was fastened on her clit. She'd had plenty of dreams such as this, but for some reason, this one felt different. The feeling was so much more intense. The orgasm that she felt coming on was about to make her lose her breath.

She woke with a start, just in time to see Eric flickering his tongue on her clit, just in time to grab his head and pull it to her as she had an out-of-body experience from his assault on her pussy with his tongue. As she began to float back down, she felt him placing kisses on her inner thighs.

"So delicious, baby," he said as he let his teeth scrape against her clit before sucking it back into his mouth. Her body buckled again as the contact sent her over the edge once more.

"Eric," she cried once she was able to speak, "what are you doing to me?"

He kissed his way up to her mouth. "I'm making love you, baby."

She had never in her wildest dreams imagined that making love to him would be this way. Her heart leaped with every kiss, every touch of his hands. She knew that she was gone, and she hoped like hell that he was sincere and serious about his needs and wants. If he were to have a change of heart, she didn't know how she would ever survive it.

She held onto him while he plunged in and out of his newly found treasure, allowing her heart to open and accept him completely.

AFTER making love in the shower, they finally had breakfast and headed out the door for work. Before letting her climb in her car, Eric attacked her mouth with a vengeance.

"You are going to make me late," she said as she pulled away from him.

"I don't care. Let's stay here today." He pulled her back to him and rocked her from side to side. He had his Kat and that was all that mattered to him at the moment.

"What about you? This is a new position and I don't think they are going to take too kindly to you missing a day already."

"Hmmm, yeah, I know. I just want to be with you. I want to spend the day loving you, making love to you." He looked deep into her eyes so that she could see that he meant every word. It was time up for the bullshit. He was making her his wife as soon as possible.

"Don't talk like that." She turned her head and looked down.

He gripped her chin and raised her head. "Why not, baby?"

"Because now I want that too," she admitted.

He put his nose in her neck and held her tightly in his arms. "Damn, Kat, you just don't know what you do to me." His hands gripped her ass.

"Eric, stop." She laughed. "Come on, let's go and get this day over with so that we can come home and finish what you have started."

"So, I can spend the night again?" His eyes twinkled. He loved the fact that she said 'we can come home.'

"Of course, you can."

"Are you sure? I don't want to be cramping your style or anything," he joked.

"I'm sure that I love having you here at all times. I'm sure that I feel safe with you here."

His heart swelled with love. She wanted him there as much as he wanted to be there. "I love being with you. I want to be with you exclusively. I want to be your man and I need for you to be my lady. Can we do that?"

Kat looked speechless for a moment. "Yes, we can do that."

He surrounded her with a tight embrace and held her for a while longer.

"Eric, we have to leave." She laughed as he nuzzled her neck.

"I know, I know. Okay, just one more kiss and then we can jet." He swooped in to claim her lips once more then released her and allowed her to get into her car before heading to his. He waited until she pulled out before following her to their job. All the while, he replayed their night in his mind.

Making love to her was unlike anything that he had ever experienced in his lifetime. He now understood what his father meant when he told him stories and gave him advice about women while they were out on the lake fishing. He knew that his dad would have loved Kat just as his mother did. For a brief moment, sadness washed over him. Then thoughts of his future wife lifted his spirits.

CHAPTER 27

KAT'S WORKDAY was going by quickly. She had a huge smile on her face all day.

"Somebody must have had some good-ass dick last night," Christy said as she propped up on Kat's desk.

"Why are you in my business?" she asked her friend while blushing.

"Naw, the question is why aren't you sharing your business?" They both laughed at that. "Come on now, for real. Let me know what the deal is. Who is the lucky man?"

"Who's to say that I'm not the lucky one?"

"Girl, if you don't cut the shit and spill, I'm going to be highly pissed off with you for a while this time." Kat laughed at Christy.

She decided that she was going to let her friend in on her new relationship. She'd been keeping a tight wrap on things, but it was bound to come out sooner or later. Especially since she'd been thinking all morning of asking him to move in with her. She wasn't sure if it was too soon or not, but she knew that she wanted them to be together.

"Okay, here's the deal, I have a man." She squealed.

"I knew it. Do I know him? Where did you guys meet?" Christy's questions tumbled out faster than Kat could answer them.

Kat held up her hands while laughing. "Girl, give me time to answer the damn questions first before asking more."

"You are taking too long. Come on and spill it."

"It's Eric." She paused to let it sink in.

Christy's eyes got big. "Oh my gosh, are you serious? Are you guys an item now?"

"Yes, we are. We made it official this morning." Kat couldn't keep the smile from spreading across her face.

"You go girl. You fucking go," Christy exclaimed

"Excuse me, Kat." A voice interrupted the two women's chat. Kat looked up and saw Trixie standing next to her desk. "I was wondering if you could help me out with this edit. I think I have everything covered, but I would appreciate it if you would double check it for me."

"Sure, I can do that." Kat told her. She was in such a good mood that she didn't stop to think about the fact that this was the first time Trixie had asked her for help. Usually, she went to the men and cajoled them into doing her work for her.

"Oh, thanks so much. I really don't want Angela on my ass about this edit. I know she is probably itching to fire my ass." Trixie gave a little laugh.

"Girl, she's itching to fire every one of our asses. I bet she gets off on the shit." Christy fell right in her trap.

Kat smiled and decided it was time to get back to her own work. "I can have this done for you before quitting time," she told Trixie and turned her attention back to her computer.

"Oh no, Miss Thang," Christy said. "You need to finish with the juice. You can't lay the man-card on me and not go into details."

"Oooh, you have a new man?" Trixie asked.

"She sure does." Christy put her hands on her hips. "And she thinks I'm going to let her get away with not spilling it."

"A secret love affair? Oh how romantic," Trixie exclaimed.

"Oh no, it is definitely not a secret. They are doing it big around here. They're all coupled up and shit."

"Come on, Kat, who's the lucky man?" Trixie looked interested.

"It's none of y'all business," Kat informed them.

Christy leaned in to Trixie and said, "It's Eric." Then she looked back at Kat and smirked.

"Eric, really?"

"Yeah, really. Why is it so hard to believe?" Kat was beginning to get offended. It was bad enough that they were all in her business, but then they were acting like it was unnatural for him to be the least bit attracted to her.

"It's just that with that incident between you two, you know, it has been like bad blood." Trixie looked around the room. She looked nervous.

"Well, we got past that and we're good."

"I'm glad y'all did," Christy said. "Girl, is he good in bed? I heard that he had a big-ass dick."

"Hey, hey. You are talking about my man, remember?"

"Girl, I'm sorry. I was just curious to know if the rumors were true at all."

Kat looked at her and shook her head. "You are a trip and you know it."

Christy wouldn't give up. "Well, are they?"

"Sorry, I don't kiss and tell."

"I'm thinking you don't kiss at all because everyone knows how Eric feels about kissing," Trixie said. "He's always said that it was gross because you never knew where the other person's mouth has been."

"That's nice to know," Kat said as she turned her attention back to her work and ignored them.

CHAPTER 28

IN THE break room, Kat was warming up lunch when she felt an arm wrap around her waist and pull her back into a rock-hard body. From the way she fit into the body and the smell of the cologne, she knew exactly who it was without having to turn around.

Eric put his face in the crook of her neck and placed a light kiss there. "I've been missing you, baby," he whispered to her, seeming oblivious to the attention they had from the other workers.

"Same here," she said as she leaned back into him.

"See, shit like that is what makes it hard for a brotha to leave your ass in the morning," he told her while nibbling on her ear.

"Eric, stop it. We are in public," she reprimanded him.

"So what? You are mine and I can do whatever I want to you and with you." His bold attitude was doing something to her nerves. She loved that shit. It had her wishing that he would do more than just talk.

"I love it when you are naughty," she told him, giving in to his embrace.

"Do you? I can be very fucking naughty if you want, baby." He pressed his dick against her ass.

She gasped. Just then the microwave beeped. "Our food is ready."

He laughed out loud and walked over to the soda machine to get them both drinks. At the table, they were in their own little world with neither one of them paying attention to the other occupants of the room.

"What time will you be home?" Kat asked Eric not really thinking about what she said.

"Home?" He looked at her expectantly.

"I'm sorry, I meant what time are you coming over to my home?" She avoided his eyes.

"As soon as I can. I am planning on stopping by the hospital to check on Tim then I'll go to my place and grab some clothes and head on over. Is that cool?"

"Yeah, that's fine. Tell Tim that I said hi." She looked up and smiled.

He smiled back and took her hand in his. "Ok, will do. I must admit that I really like the way you keep referring to your house as our home." He cocked his head to the side.

"I do not keep doing that." She felt the heat creeping in her cheeks. She let her eyes wander around the room before returning to meet his.

"Yes, you do, but it's all good. I'm cool with that." He raised her hand to his mouth and placed a kiss on her palm.

"What if I said that I wanted you there at all times?" The kiss made her bold and she spoke what was on her mind.

"What if I said that I wanted to be there at all times?" His eyes seemed to challenge her.

"I would be thrilled." She let her hand cover his.

"So are you asking me?"

"What if I am?" She was nervous as hell. What if he said no? What if she was pushing him away with being so needy?

"Well then, I guess I will need to get more than just a few things." He leaned his head to the side slightly. "Maybe I need to get as much as possible in that one trip and then get the rest over the weekend."

Kat's heart thumped loudly in her chest. He said yes. She wanted to jump up and down and scream for joy, but she couldn't. Instead, she let a huge grin take over her face. "That sounds like a plan to me." His face mirrored her own, a huge grin plastered on his face also.

After they finished lunch, Kat walked Eric to the elevator so that he could return to his floor. He pulled her past the elevator and into the door where the stairs were.

"What are you doing, Eric?" She giggled as he forced her up against the wall.

"I'm stealing a kiss," he told her as his mouth claimed hers in a greedy kiss. His tongue slipped past her lips and began to caress hers.

She moaned into his mouth and felt his arms tighten around her. Her arms flew around his neck and pulled him closer.

"Kat, you drive me so fucking insane, you know that? I'm so glad that you are finally all mine." He placed little kisses on her neck.

She could feel his dick pressing against her stomach. And she wanted it so bad. "You have to stop this. It's not fair," she whined.

"Why not, baby? You want your dick, love?"

"Yes, I want it. I need it bad." She let her lips brush against his neck.

"Come upstairs with me, baby," he insisted.

"I can't."

"You can. I will send for you once you clock back in. Then come to me."

"Okay."

He gave her another deep kiss before leading her out of the stairwell.

Trixie could not believe it. Kat had the look of a woman who had been seriously turned on. Her pupils were dilated and her lips were swollen from kisses she assumed. Kisses that everyone assumed Eric did not like. She even saw a few passion marks on Kat's neck. She couldn't believe it. He had passed on her and went to the one woman that he claimed to not want. Everybody knew that he despised Kat. They all knew that she was not the kind of woman he was attracted to. So why was he suddenly all into her?

She vowed to find out what was really going on. She had a thing for Eric and would not play second to anyone. Especially not to some fat ass goody-two-shoes bitch who didn't know shit about the real world. She looked over at Kat and saw her smiling to herself. Trixie felt disgusted. That woman was wearing the smile that should have been hers.

Shit, she had put in work to make it happen. Her kids needed a daddy, and Eric was daddy-material. He had a nice bank account, a decent job, a nice ride, and a damn fine-ass body. She could definitely deal. But now, this bitch wanted to rain on her parade. She had to get her out of the way as soon as possible. It was almost time to start shopping for Christmas and she needed money to make ends meet. She wanted Eric's money, and if she couldn't have it, then she knew exactly where to get the extra money from. She knew of another person with things to hide and an agenda to match her own.

CHAPTER 29

KAT RECEIVED a message from Eric telling her to make her way to his office. Her pussy jumped in anticipation of the orgasm she knew was waiting for her on the seventh floor. Pretending to be going to a meeting, she headed to the elevators. She ran into Angela on the way.

"Where are you going?" Angela asked her.

"I have a meeting that I need to attend," Kat said.

"Kat, I'm not stupid. I saw you exit the stairwell with Eric. I know you are going to see him."

"Yeah, I am going to see him." She was tired of playing around with this chick. "Do you have a problem with that?"

"You know I could fire your ass for messing around on the job, right?"

Kat crossed her arms and shifted to one side. "You could do that, but then you would have some explaining to do yourself, being that you are the one that showed me it was okay to 'mess around on the job' as you say. I recall the first time that you ate my pussy was in this office. I also recall the little setup you had for me and Eric. It would be a pity if I have to go there with you."

"You think you are slick, but I got you, baby girl. I refuse to let him have all of the fun. You will be back. Just watch and see." Angela turned and walked away.

Kat wasted no time in going to Eric's office. There, she knocked on the door and waited until she heard him tell her to enter.

"You called for me, sir?"

He looked at her before answering. "Yes, ma'am, I did. Why don't you come around here and sit on my desk?"

She looked around. "Umm, I don't know if that is a good idea. What if someone walks in?"

He got up from his chair and walked to the door. After locking it, he walked over to her and brushed her hair from her face and let his hand slide down her body to her waist. "I heard that you have doubted me and my abilities."

"I don't know what you are talking about, sir. I think that you are a great boss. I would never cross you," she told him, playing along.

"I need you to prove your loyalty to me." His hand made its way to her ass and he gave it a squeeze. "Why don't you remove your dress for me?"

"I don't—" Before she could finish, he smacked her on her rear.

"Now," he demanded. He stepped back and sat down in one of the chairs meant for guests. She faced him and slowly removed her dress, moving to a tune playing in her head.

"Simply beautiful," he said as he rubbed himself. She could see that his dick was rock hard and she wanted it.

"What shall I do now?" she asked him in a low voice.

"Lay across my desk with that phat ass pointing towards me."

Kat did as he instructed. As soon as she was in the desired position, she felt his hands on her thighs. She needed him inside of her in the worst way. The ache was almost unbearable for her. She felt his lips on one of her cheeks while his hands were exploring her body. She heard clothing rustle then felt him rub the tip of his dick on her ass cheeks. She bit her lip.

"Eric, I need you, Daddy," she pleaded.

"You are so wet, baby." His hands continued to wander. "You want me, love?" he asked.

"Yes," she moaned.

He entered her with a force so great that she lost her breath. As he stroked her, she lay on his desk in pure bliss. It seemed to her that with each and every stroke he was laying claim to her body, heart, and soul.

Neither said a word while they rode the wave of ecstasy. He drove his dick deep and kept it there while rotating his hips. As she felt her orgasm creeping through her body, he pulled her up to his chest and sucked on her neck, while she screamed with pleasure. After she was spent, he dived in one final time and stiffened, spilling his seed into her womb.

"I love you," he whispered.

"I love you too," she said.

"You promise?" His voice was needy.

"I promise that I love you and I will keep on loving you forever," she told him as he held on to her like his life depended on it.

It was at that moment she saw that her love was what he craved, what he needed to continue surviving. She knew that she was his savior as he was hers.

They cleaned themselves and stood in an embrace at his door, Eric not releasing her yet.

"My beautiful, Kat, you have no idea how much I need you, how much I love you." His eyes bored into her soul. "I have always known you were the one," he told her.

With those words, she finally had the answers to all of her questions.

Leaving Eric's office, Kat realized that all of those feelings she had for him from the start were reciprocated as she had thought. She wasn't crazy feeling like he was the man for her. They just had a major flaw thrown in their mix, his mother's death being the biggest. But even after that, they'd still managed to find their way to one another. He was her soul mate. All the dreams she'd had of him were premonitions, not just wants or desires.

She walked back to her desk with renewed energy, determined that nothing and no one would ever come between them.

TRIXIE saw Kat's glow and the contentment on her face. It sent her into a rage. She watched Kat for the rest of the day. She had to eliminate her.

That bitch would pay for stealing her man.

CHAPTER 30

ERIC WENT straight to the hospital after work. When he got to Tim's room, he saw that a few of his family members were there, including his mother.

"Hey, man, it's good to see you sitting up." He walked over to the bed and gave his friend a hug.

"Man, it's good to be able to sit up," Tim said. "I'm just thankful that I'm still on this earth, to tell you the truth."

"I know what you mean." He was glad for his boy too. He said a silent prayer and gave thanks for the miracle.

"So, how was your day?" Tim asked. He cocked his head to the side and grinned. He gestured toward Eric's neck. "I guess I can see how it went."

Eric blushed and cleared his throat. He pulled a vacant chair up next to the bed and sat down. "It was cool. Busy as heck, but cool."

Tim laughed. "Yeah. I can tell you've been getting busy."

"Where's Kat," asked Mama Bee.

"She should be home. As a matter of fact, I'm heading over there after I leave here." He glanced at his watch.

"Man, you can go on and spend time with your girl," Tim said, "I'm good. You can hit me up later."

Eric shook his head. "Dude, I came to check up on you and you're trying to throw me out already?" He chuckled.

"We aren't trying to throw you out," Momma Bee told him, "but we do want you to go and be with your lady. You have been waiting on this moment for so long. Now that it is here, don't mess it up."

"Kat is fine with me being here. It is really not a problem. She knows that Tim is my best friend. She even told me to tell y'all hi."

"Tell her we said hello," Tim said. "And I know all of that, but what I am telling you is go get your woman. Go have dinner with her and whisper sweet nothings in her ear. Time is too precious. Believe me, I know. Go and make it happen for you guys, and the next time I see you, I want to see her with you, understand?"

Eric laughed. "Man, you must be on that Morphine."

Tim lay back down. "Naw, I'm just glad that you found your soul mate. Life is too precious to be wasting it on doubts and procrastinations."

"When are you going to marry her?" Momma Bee asked Eric.

He stood up. "I don't know yet, but I am working on it." He gave her a hug and gave Tim some dap before leaving the room, promising them he would tell Kat they said hi.

As soon as he pulled into the garage, Kat threw the door open and walked out. Even in casual house clothes, she still was his beautiful Kat. He hopped out of the car and walked towards her. She jumped into his arms. He held her close to him for a moment before letting their lips connect. After a tantalizing kiss, she pulled away from him and looked in his car.

"Yes," Eric said, "I did bring some of my things. I told you I would."

She smiled up at him. "I'm glad you didn't change your mind."

"Never that, baby. I want this love. I've wanted this for a long time, so no worries babe, no doubts. I'm moving in the right direction." He knew that he was finally home. With Kat was where he was meant to be and where he planned on staying.

She helped him carry his things into the house and put them away before returning to the kitchen to start dinner. This was his first night in his new home with his love. He helped her make a special candlelight dinner, complete with a bottle of wine and soft music playing in the background. After dinner, they shared a long soak in the tub followed by each giving one another a sensual massage. They went to bed early that night, even though sleep was the last thing on either one of their minds.

Eric's mind was on branding Kat and claiming her heart. They made love over and over that night with Kat falling asleep in his arms, her head on his chest.

At one point, it seemed as if their hearts were beating as one. Eric finally felt complete.

CHAPTER 31

ERIC DIDN'T try to hide his affection for Kat. Everyone in the office could see that he was totally in love with her. Every week, when the delivery guy from the floral shop arrived, they knew it was for her. Whenever he made an appearance in the break room, he was with her.

He had even started to cut his fun time with his friends down and spent most of his free time with Kat. She was the most important person in his life and he planned on keeping it that way. He loved her and that was all he was concerned with. Time seemed to stand still when he was with her. He wanted all she had to give. He enjoyed their life together and he was ready for more.

While out with Tim, he found the perfect ring for her. Tim told him that if he felt like she was the right woman and it was the right ring, then he should go ahead and get it. It was the best money he'd ever spent.

He kept the ring in a safe place, awaiting the day to give it to his love. He was too nervous to pop the question. Eric did not want them bringing any negativity into their marriage. He wanted to be absolutely sure Kat was ready. Although he knew Angela was a thorn from the past, he still thought of their relationship from time to time.

Eric loved being in a serious relationship. He loved waking up wrapped in Kat's arms. He loved the showers they shared, the late night movies, everything. Kat complemented him in every way imaginable. She was his match, and being with her was an absolute delight for him. He knew that this was it. His playa's card had officially been revoked. He was smitten and that is all there was to it.

His days were full of smiles and his nights were full of exquisite pleasure. His heart was full of love and Kat made sure that his stomach was full also.

CHAPTER 32

KAT WAS happy, completely happy for the first time in her life. Things between her and Eric were wonderful. She loved having him home with her. They mostly spent the weekends at home, fixing up the place to her liking. They would lie on the oversized couch at night and watch movies until it was bedtime. She never knew being in love would be like that. She was never tired of him and it seemed he was never tired of her.

They had their disagreements like every other couple, but the good outweighed the little spats. In her heart, she knew it was only a matter of time before he proposed. She knew that she was ready for more; she just had to wait for him to get to that point. They had not spoken of marriage, even though he wanted her to have his baby. They no longer used protection in hopes of becoming pregnant. She was ready to have his babies, as many as he wanted.

Sometimes Kat and Eric rode to work together, but on the days when he had to work late, they went in different cars. This day they had decided on each driving because his team had a big assignment to complete. She was proud of the progress he was making at the company. He had quickly become a top manager with people trying to transfer to his department. He had often asked her to put in a transfer, but she knew that it wouldn't be wise and that Angela wouldn't approve it. Even though Angela kept her distance, Kat could still feel the pissed-off looks her boss threw her way.

On the way in, she had noticed a few people looking at her strangely and wondered what was going on. She had looked in the mirror to see if she had something out of the ordinary on her face, but nothing was there. She brushed it off and was ready to begin her workday. As soon as she sat at her desk, she logged in to her computer. It dinged, letting her know that she had a message. It was a mass message that was sent to all of the employees.

When she opened it, her whole world stopped. It felt like the wind had been knocked from her and she thought she might pass out. On the screen were pictures of her and Angela in the middle of a very intense sexual act. She must have had a camera set up, because every angle was a clear image of Kat, but not her. No one else would be able to tell it was Angela, but she knew. Somebody had captured them in the act, and now that someone had sent the pictures to every employee in the building.

Kat didn't know what to do, but she knew she had to do something. As she sat there, her humiliation turned to anger. She stood up from her desk and, holding her head high, marched straight to her boss's office and barged in without knocking. There, she let loose of all of the fury she was feeling.

"You fucking bitch, how could you do this to me?" she demanded as she stood over Angela.

Angela sat back in her chair and crossed her arms. "What are you talking about?"

"You know what I'm talking about," Kat screamed. She slammed a fist on the desk. "You fucking sent pictures to every one of you between my legs. You took pictures of me without me knowing it."

Angela hit the intercom button and yelled for her secretary to call security. She jumped up from her chair and backed away from Kat.

"Kat, I promise you that I have no idea what you are talking about. Just calm down."

"So, am I supposed to believe that you don't know what the hell is going on? Do you think I'm fucking stupid?" Kat picked up a paperweight from the desk and was about to hit Angela with it when a security guard caught her from behind. She saw relief flash across Angela's face. "Bitch, I'm going to fucking kill you." She struggled to get loose from the guard.

"I need you leave this building now," Angela shouted.

"Screw you," Kat threw out at her as she broke free from the guards and walked back to her desk. She began gathering her belongings while the guards stood by and watched her. Angela stood outside of her office watching.

As Kat was getting the last of her things, the image popped back up on her screen. She was lying on her back with her legs spread wide open while a woman feasted on her. She was completely nude and her eyes were closed. She grabbed the monitor and threw it against the wall. There were gasps heard around the room as the monitor exploded. The guards grabbed her before she could do any more damage.

Eric burst through the door just in time to see them dragging

Kat out of the office. He raced over to them and pushed them away from her. He took her in his arms, picked up her things, and led her to the elevators. Neither said a word until they made it to the parking garage. It was then that she broke down. He held her while she cried.

"Mark called and told me to get down there quick. What happened, Kat?" His voice was soothing to her fragile spirit.

"Oh, Eric," she sniffled as she held on to him. "There were these pictures of me and Angela."

"What do you mean?"

"They were of us in her bed." She put her head to his chest and cried harder.

"Shhh, Kat. I got you." He rubbed her back. "It's going to be okay."

"It's not okay. Everybody knows. They saw my body, they saw everything." She started sobbing and couldn't continue.

Eric guided her to her car, helped her inside, and drove her home. He called his boss to let him know what had transpired. He sympathized with their situation and said they were working on finding out who had done such a horrible thing. He told Eric to take care of Kat and ended the conversation.

Kat stayed in bed for the rest of the day. She could not believe that everyone now knew of her lesbian love affair. Her feelings for Angela turned into pure hatred. She hoped that the pictures would not affect her relationship with Eric. She was finally happy and now this had to happen.

Finally tired of wallowing in self-pity, she got up and went to shower. Afterward, she went downstairs in search of Eric. She found him in the kitchen making some sandwiches.

"Hi, beautiful, how are you feeling?" he asked when he saw her.

"I feel like I have been run over by a truck," she said as she walked up to him and wrapped her arms around his waist.

"Do you need for me to get you an aspirin?" He held her with his chin resting on her head.

"No, I'm fine. This right here is all that I need at the moment."

"You know that I love you, right?" he said.

"Yes, I do."

"Nothing will ever change that. Nothing. We will get through this together."

"Thank you for loving me." She squeezed him. "You are the best thing that has ever happened to me."

"So are you, and I'll be damned if I let anyone destroy what we have found. Always remember that, Kat."

He kissed her and before she knew it, she was back in the bed. But this time, she was no longer distraught. Instead of tears of pain and hurt, this time, she wept tears of pure ecstasy.

CHAPTER 33

THE NEWS of Kat's lesbian affair went beyond the workplace. Someone even sent a copy of the pictures to her mother. Eric gave her the time and space she needed to cope with things, but he was there when she needed him.

One day as she was sitting out in the back yard reading a book, she heard a car pull up. Eric had just gone in the house to get a bottle of wine for them to drink, so she decided to let him deal with the unannounced visitor.

"Katlynn." She looked up when she heard her mother's pissed-off tone. She knew that she was going to have to deal with her sooner or later, but she had been putting it off, knowing how her mother felt about homosexuality.

She stood and faced her mother. "Yes, ma'am?"

"Why haven't you returned any of my calls?"

"I'm sorry. I have been sort of busy dealing with things."

"But not sorry enough to get your ass caught with some slut between your legs? I can't believe you would do something so damn nasty. How could you? You know that you are going to hell for partaking in such a scandalous act. And then you brought the shit back to us, in our home. How could you? I know I raised you better than that. And now you got this boy caught up in your mess. Are you trying to destroy his life too? You are nothing but a no-good hussy."

"Mom, please. I am really not in the mood." On the verge of tears, Kat felt her temper rising. She had never disrespected her mother, but she did not know how long she could hold her tongue. She already had enough to deal with. The least her mother could do was have her back and help her through this difficult time. Instead, all she got from her was negativity.

"Oh, you aren't in the mood? Well, you should have thought about that before you let some bitch share your bed. I don't want you back at my house. We don't need your disgusting ways tainting everyone else in the family."

Eric intervened. He pulled Kat to him and held her as he spoke to her mother. "I am very sorry that we are having our second meeting like this. I know you are hurt by what has happened, but Kat is hurt too. She needs your support, not your evil words. And if you cannot be there for her and offer her some sort of comfort, I am going to have to ask you to leave."

"You cannot talk to me like that. This is my daughter's house, you can't make me leave."

"I can and I will. Kat is my priority, and if you are here to cause her more pain, then I will not allow it. This is our home, Kat and I. We are happy here, and if you can't accept that and move past everything else, then it is best for you to go. Come on, love, let's go inside." He took Kat's hand and they walked in the house, leaving her mother standing there with her mouth open.

"I'm sorry that I spoke to your mother that way," he said when they got inside. "I couldn't stand there and let her hurt you like that." He hugged her tightly.

"Thank you for that. You saved me from doing the one thing that I hate, and that is disrespecting one's parents. I was so close to going off on her. I can't believe the things she said to me."

"Don't focus on that, baby. She will eventually come around and realize that she was wrong. Until then, I got you and I will always be right here for you." He lowered his head and captured her lips.

As time passed and the novelty of the pictures wore off, Kat returned to her normal fun-loving self. Eric had convinced her that he would handle all of the bills. All that he wanted to do was focus her attention on being happy, centering herself, and doing whatever it was that brought her joy. He had even suggested she take up some classes if she wanted to. She was thrilled at the idea of going back to school. Even though she didn't admit it to anyone, she was delighted to be able to be staying at home for a while.

CHAPTER 34

IT HAD been a couple of months since the pictures. Tim's mother convinced Kat to accept an invitation to Tim's birthday bash. It was mostly all family with a few close friends of the family. The older lady finally won out when she told Kat that whatever she did in her past was no one's business except for Eric and her. And as long as he was still by her side, the rest of the world shouldn't matter to her.

Eric spent majority of the day watching Kat interact with Tim's family. He was so engrossed in his observation that he didn't hear Tim walk up beside him.

"Damn, man, you got it bad, huh?"

"Yeah, I do. Man, I think that it is time," Eric said. He was ready to take that final step.

"Do you think she will say yes?"

"I don't know. At first, I felt like she would have, but now, with all of the shit that's been going on, I really don't know." His thoughts went back to the pictures that had turned their world upside down in a matter of minutes.

"Maybe you should wait a little while longer until all of this shit blows over," Tim told Eric.

"I don't know. Why should we have to put our lives on hold just because some jealous-ass freak wants to get their two minutes of fame? I think we should go on with our lives and let them know that they aren't going to win."

"I hear you, but does Kat feel the same way?"

"She doesn't really want to talk about it. Her family had been giving her a hard time and all. I wish I could punch everybody that hurts her in the fucking face just once." His hands balled into fists.

"That would not be good. Then your ass would be in trouble and wouldn't be there to protect her for real."

"Yeah, I know. That's the only reason that I haven't acted on it yet. Man, do you know that nigga Mark had the nerve to tell me that he couldn't believe that I was strung out over her chunky ass. I swear it took everything in me not to fuck him up." Eric's eyes were hard with anger.

"No shit? I don't understand why you hang out with that dude. He is a hater to the fullest. I know you wanted to beat his ass."

"Yeah, I did. And I know it's fucked up to admit it, but I know that I'm going to have to get him one of these days. I feel it deep down in my bones. I can't understand why the hell they are all in our business. Why is it necessary for them to offer their opinions when they aren't needed or wanted?" His eyes found Kat again and his look softened.

"Maybe y'all need a little getaway, just for a piece of mind."

"You know what, that is exactly what I'm going to do. A vacation is a great idea right about now. Hey, thanks, man." Kat had never been on a real vacation before. Maybe a getaway was just what she needed. He shook hands with Tim and gave him a brotherly hug before making his way over to his love. He walked up behind her and wrapped his arms around her waist. "Hey, gorgeous. Are you having fun?"

She leaned back against him. "It's nice here. Everyone is so sweet." He felt the tension leaving her body.

"That's good. I'm glad you decided to come with me."

"Thanks for making me come. I really needed to get out of the house for a while." She turned toward him and eased her hands up his chest to his neck.

"How about if we go on a mini vacation?"

"Where would we go?"

"Anywhere you want, love."

"I have always wanted to go to Jamaica. Or maybe to Paris. What do you think?"

Eric laughed at her enthusiasm. His heart skipped a beat as he looked at the joy on her face. "I told you that we can go wherever you want. You pick the place. I don't care as long as I can be wrapped inside of them thunder thighs you have."

"Eric." She smirked.

"You know I love you, girl. You and them thick-ass thighs of yours." He drew her into his arms and gave her a quick kiss. He wanted more than that little peck, but they were surrounded by people and he had to maintain control. "Come and dance with me," he said as he pulled her to the dancing area.

After a few hours, they said their goodbyes and headed out.

"So, have you been thinking of where you want to go?" Eric asked as they went upstairs.

"Not really. We can do it together. You know, compare prices and all of that," she said as she went into the bathroom to shower.

They both continued to chat about their trip as they undressed.

Eric followed behind her. "I don't care about the price; just make sure that it's somewhere that you really want to visit." Kat smiled at him and pulled him into the shower with her. "Why are you looking at me like that?" he said as he began rubbing soap over her body.

"No reason." She licked her lips.

"Hmmmm….I'm thinking that we should start a family now."

"Are you in a rush?" She teased him with her hands.

"No, but the process of making one is oh so lovely."

"You are going to get it regardless." She smiled at him. "So tell me, are you in a rush?"

"Not necessarily a rush, but I do want us to start our family."

"We are not married." That was the first time that she had brought up marriage to him.

"We can be," he said without missing a beat.

"When, after the kid is born and you decide propose?"

"No, we can get married whenever you like, preferably before our child is born. I don't want to have a long engagement." He continued washing her body. Kat stood still, looking at him. He knew she was surprised by his admission. "Come on, Kat," he said. "Turn around and let me wash your back, baby."

"Oh, okay." She turned and let him continue with his care of her.

When he finished, he stood while she washed him. He loved the feel of her hands on his body. He was hard as steel and he needed her, but he allowed her to take her time and set their speed. He knew it would be well worth the wait.

After their shower, they went to bed with thoughts of starting a family on both of their minds.

CHAPTER 35

KAT WAS really enjoying being at home, but she knew that she needed to find a job. She didn't think it was fair to let Eric carry the weight by himself. True, he said that it was cool and he had everything under control. He wouldn't even allow her to use her savings to help out. She guessed that she was truly on her way to being a housewife. She kept house and had dinner ready for him every day. She catered to him to the best of her abilities and she enjoyed every second of it.

She remembered how her homegirls used to complain about cleaning, cooking, and just taking care of their men, but she didn't see the problem. Eric took care of her in return. They did different things, but it all came together to make a whole unit. He went to work and worked long hours. She stayed home and cleaned or what have you. When he came home, he was able to relax and release the stress from the day's work. Kat knew how demanding his job was, being that she used to work there also. Whenever he had to bring work home, she would be in the office with him helping with it.

Seeing an advertisement for a Caribbean cruise, she turned

up the volume on the TV. It looked romantic and fun, so she grabbed her laptop to look it up. She saved the information to show it to Eric when he came home. She hoped that it wasn't too expensive. They could even go half on it.

After dinner, she pulled up the site to show him her discovery.

"Wow, that looks nice." he exclaimed while looking through the pictures of the rooms and destinations.

"I know. It is beautiful, isn't it? Can we take this cruise? We can get the cheapest rooms and we can go half on it." Eric howled with laughter. She frowned. He was laughing so hard that tears had formed in his eyes. "I really don't see what's so darn funny," she told him.

"Wait…." He could hardly speak because of the laughter. "Kat, I told you we could go wherever you wanted to go. It's cool."

"Okay, so why are you so tickled?"

"Because your sales talk is weak as hell. I mean, I appreciate the effort, but damn, baby, you need to work on it a little bit more."

"Forget you, dude." She stood up and put her hands on her hips. "Don't front. I was just trying to be nice and let you know that I got you."

"You got me, babe?" He reached for her.

"No, you are in trouble," she told him as he pulled her between his legs. "Don't be trying to change the conversation."

He let his hands glide underneath her blouse and up to her breasts. His fingers twirled her nipples while he looked up into her eyes. "Hmmmm…. See, you should have started with this, and I would have definitely said yes to whatever you wanted."

"Anything?" Her nipples were hard as pebbles and she felt the throbbing start between her legs.

"Yes, anything." He released her breasts and slid his hands to the waistband of her shorts. Opening the buttons with his teeth was his specialty and she enjoyed watching him do it. He pulled them and her panties down at the same time. All the while, he held her gaze.

"I'm ready for my dessert," he told her as he sat her on the table in front of him. His eyes were full of desire.

He traced her inner thighs with his nose then gripped her thighs before indulging in the sweetness. He took his time and lapped up all of her juices. Her clit was the focus of his attention and he placed lavish kisses all around the bud.

Kat's moans grew louder until she no longer could utter a word. The pleasure he gave her would not allow her to speak, let alone breathe.

When he was done feasting on her pussy, he pulled her from the table and told her to turn around and bend over. He entered her as slow as possible and stroked her nice and slow while whispering words of love to her. Then he picked up speed and held on to her as he rode her to ecstasy and back. The harder he stroked, the more she threw it back. On and on until they were both spent.

"Did you enjoy that babe?" he asked afterward as he held her in a loving embrace.

"Yes, you know I did." Her head was on his chest and she was listening to the beat of his heart.

"Do you want more, love?"

"Always."

He took her hand and led her up the stairs to their bedroom, where he took his time making love to her for the rest of the night.

CHAPTER 36

ERIC WAS researching the cruise that Kat wanted to take when an idea came to him. He called a travel agency and got the information he was looking for. His heart thumped loudly as he made the arrangements and started the process. He probably should have asked her first before changing the cruise, but he didn't think about it at the time. He was too amped with what he had discovered.

He could hardly concentrate on his work. All he could think about was if everything went according to plan, this time next month, his mother would get her wish. He smiled to himself as he tried to focus on his computer screen for the umpteenth time that day. He was ready to see his Kat.

When he made it home, he decided it was best if he went ahead and explained the situation to her before it was time to leave. As they were snuggled up on the couch, watching a TV show, he told her about the change.

"Hey, baby, I changed our vacation," he began.

She looked up at him. "Oh yeah?"

"Yeah, I saw this other one online and I think that you'd enjoy it more. We would be going to Bermuda instead of the Caribbean. The rooms will be the same, but instead of it being just for five days, we will have seven." He got up from the couch and grabbed his laptop to show her.

"Oh my goodness, this is absolutely beautiful," she exclaimed as she looked through the site. "Wow, it is gorgeous and expensive. You didn't have to get that particular one. I'm not saying that I don't appreciate it, it's just that you are taking care of everything and now you are paying for this cruise."

"You don't worry about any of that. I got you, love. If I didn't, I would let you know. As of now, you have nothing to worry about. All I want for you to do is be happy and plan for our trip." He traced her jawline with one finger.

"You are so good to me."

"I am only just beginning. You should wait until you are my wife." He winked at her then went to the kitchen.

CHAPTER 37

KAT WAS in love with the cruise ship. She and Eric had a wonderful time touring each place they docked at. She took a ton of pictures for her scrapbook. The different gardens Eric found just for her were simply breathtaking. She was in awe of the amount of detail he had put into researching the trip. He had their days mapped out. All she had to do was get dressed and follow his lead. Whenever they weren't sightseeing, they were making love in various places.

Everywhere they went, people smiled in their direction. The little old couple that shared the dinner table with them told them that their auras were beautiful together and that was why they drew attention from others. At night, they took long walks on the ship's deck and enjoyed the view. They had a room with a balcony, so they spent time sipping fine wine and watching the stars out there. Kat felt completely at peace.

On the last night of the cruise, they dressed for the formal dinner. Eric was in the shower when she heard a knock on the door. A woman was there with a couple of packages for her.

"What is this?"

"This is for you to wear tonight."

"I didn't order anything," Kat told the lady while taking the packages.

"No, but your beau did," the lady informed her with a sparkle in her eyes. "I hope you find everything to your liking. If there are any problems, just call the shop and I can have something else brought up for you. Enjoy your night." She raised her eyebrows and smiled before turning to leave.

Kat closed the door and sat on the bed to open the packages. She couldn't believe her eyes. Inside one was the most gorgeous dress she had ever seen. Her heart swelled with love at the thought of Eric shopping for her. He knew that her favorite color was purple and the dress that he had chosen was a lovely grape-colored Vera Wang piece. The fabric flowed from a silver belt underneath the bust line and hung to the floor. It looked every bit of a wedding dress. She decided not mention it to him, though, because the dress was gorgeous. The shoes that he had chosen were silver to match the belt. She loved everything about the whole ensemble.

"I see your gifts have arrived," she heard Eric say from behind her.

She jumped up and flew into his arms. "Oh, Eric, it is all so beautiful," she exclaimed.

"A beautiful dress for a beautiful lady," he told her. His arms tightened around her waist.

"You are going to make me cry and ruin my makeup."

She put on her new dress, the gorgeous dress that she had picked out to wear long forgotten. Eric helped her with her jewelry and then stood back to look at her.

"You are the most beautiful woman in the world to me," he said after a minute.

"And you, good sir, are the most beautiful man I have ever had the pleasure of meeting." She smiled at him. He was dressed to kill as always; his tailored black suit fit him perfectly. His silk shirt matched her dress.

He reached out one arm to her. "Shall we?"

She took the arm that was offered and said, "We shall."

CHAPTER 38

WHEN THEY entered the banquet hall, Kat's breathing stopped. She looked around the room to take in the splendor of it. Each table had a bouquet of purple and white Calla Lilies and some green flowers that she didn't know the name of as the centerpiece. The color scheme for the night seemed to be purple. An archway at the front of the room was lined with more purple Calla Lilies.

Eric led her towards the front of the room where Mrs. and Mr. Dubois, the older couple they had met were seated. Kat noticed the way people were looking at them and wondered if something was on her face or if she was having a clothing malfunction.

"Relax, Kat," Eric whispered. "They are admiring your radiant beauty. Did you know that you are glowing, my love?"

"Really?" She looked to him for an answer.

His eyes held hers for a moment before he answered her. "Yes. I am beginning to wonder if you are carrying my seed." He smiled smugly.

"Why do you say that?"

"Because it is true and we will find out as soon as we return home."

She smiled at the thought of having his seed growing inside of her. "I'm so in love with you." She told him. He continued smiling at her as the captain asked for everyone's attention.

"This is a very special night, one that we are glad to share with each and every one of you. At the start of this journey, a young man came to me with a request. I must admit that I thought it might not work out the way that he wanted it to, but after observing him and his lady friend for the duration of this trip, I wholeheartedly agree with his plan."

Kat became aware that her favorite song had started playing in the background. A hush fell over the hall as Eric stood up next to her and then got down on one knee. Tears sprang to her eyes.

"Kat, my beautiful Kat. I have been in love with you ever since the moment I first saw you. You are the love of my life, my soul mate, my all. You make each day worth living. In my time of need, you were there for me. You are my strength when I am weak. You are my light in my moments of darkness. You are my voice of reason during my insanity. With you, I feel as if I can conquer the world; just as long as I have you by my side. I need you in my life forever. Tonight, I am asking you to become one with me. Marry me right here, right now, on this beautiful cruise ship. Let this be the start of our happily ever after."

She was speechless.

"Say yes, honey," Mrs. Dubois said. The other passengers laughed.

"Yes, Eric, I will marry you."

He stood. "Right here, right now?"

She smiled and nodded and he pulled her to him and kissed her in front of everyone.

"Shall we begin?" the captain asked.

"Yes, sir," Eric replied as he walked a stunned Kat to the stage. They stood underneath the arch she had admired earlier.

While the other cruise passengers looked on, they were united as husband and wife.

EVERYTHING had worked out wonderfully. Eric had hired a wedding planner and she had followed his instructions word for word. The couple celebrated with the other passengers until late into the night. Ready to have his new wife to himself, Eric led her back to their room and made slow passionate love to her as if it was their first time all over again.

The next day when she finally woke up, he had their belongings packed and sitting by the door.

"What's going on?" she asked him sleepily.

"The ship will be leaving soon, so we have to get off here," he told her.

"Why do we have to get off? I thought we were heading home?" She sat up in bed and looked at her husband.

"No, love, we just got married. Now it is time for our honeymoon in Bermuda to begin." He climbed back in bed with her and pulled her to him.

"Oh, Eric, I can't believe you did all of this without me knowing about it."

"Are you enjoying it?"

"How could I not? This is all like a fairy tale and you are my knight in shining armor, my Prince Charming, and all of that." She caressed his face as he leaned in to kiss her.

"I love you, Mrs. Lefevre."

She smiled at him. "I love you too, Mr. Lefevre."

She pulled him to her and they spent the remainder of their time aboard the ship wrapped in one another's arms.

When the couple left the ship, they headed straight to the hotel where they would be staying.

"I must confess," Eric said, "the reason why I was so hell bent on exploring before was because I am planning on holding you hostage in this room. We can go out some if you like, but I plan on ravishing you the entire time."

"I don't think that is such a bad idea. In fact, I am glad you thought so far ahead. I'm ready for all you have in store." She slid down the straps of her dress and letting the material pool around her feet. She heard his sharp intake of breath when he saw her barely-there thong.

"Damn," he said as he made his way to her. He picked her up and carried her to the bed.

CHAPTER 39

TRUE TO Eric's words, he and Kat spent most of their time locked in their hotel room. They did venture out at times, but never for long. She begged him to take her to the botanical garden again and he gave in after making her promise to do something for him which involved him tying her to the bed. The gardens gave her plenty of ideas for her own one at home. She took notes and told Eric of her plans and he agreed to help her with them. She knew he enjoyed helping her in the yard. It was always just them and nature.

When the time came for them to leave, they were both exhausted, mentally and physically, but both were extremely happy and completely sated. Kat had her husband and Eric had his wife. They would return home as one.

Kat looked at Eric. "I am going to miss this place."

"Me too. It has been wonderful having you all to myself with no interruptions at all. A man could get used to this." He smiled as he pulled her to him. He caressed her cheek before leaning down to capture her bottom lip.

"Ummm…My naughty husband," she moaned into his mouth.

"My luscious wife," he said as he slipped his tongue between her lips.

"Eric, don't start something you won't be able to finish," Kat told him as she pulled away from him.

"Oh, you know for sure that I can finish it," Eric boasted. He grabbed her by the hands and pulled her to the bathroom.

"Eric," she whined as she followed him.

"I think you missed a spot on your back earlier. I'm just going to get it for you right quick." He smiled in her direction as they entered the bathroom.

"Oh, is that right? Well, in that case, we definitely need to take care of that."

She started to undress while he turned on the shower. He turned and watched her, his eyes hooded and full of desire as he watched her striptease. When she was completely nude, she made her way over to him and began to relieve him of his clothes.

He hissed when her hands closed around him and started moving against the silky skin of his hard shaft. Her pink tongue darted out of her mouth and flickered across his nipple.

"Fuck," he cried between his gritted teeth.

Kat smiled against his chest, delighted that she had this control over such a beautiful man. She was just about to drop to her knees and take him into her mouth when he stopped her. "I can't take much more, baby. I need to be inside of you." He pulled her closer to him, lifting her up so that her soft spot was where he wanted it to be.

She wanted more. She wrapped one leg around his waist. He entered the shower. Pushing her up against the wall, he entered her wetness slowly while capturing one of her taut chocolate nipples between his lips. She threw her head back and moaned as his hands and mouth worked her over, helping bring her to the top of the mountain. Eric found her sensitive spot on her neck and sucked. Her body started to shake and she called out his name. He went over the edge at the same time.

Both spent and out of breath, they looked one another in the eyes, promising to love each other forever and always.

CHAPTER 40

WHEN THE couple got home from their trip, Eric carried Kat over the threshold as she laughed at him. No one knew of their wedding aboard the ship, and that was the way they both preferred it. With Kat's family not really speaking to her, that decision was not a hard one for her to make. So, when she checked their messages and heard her mom's voice, she knew there would be a few more months of silence from her mother because of not knowing about the wedding.

"Are you okay?" Eric asked her as he walked up behind her.

"I know my mom is about to continue with the silent treatment once I tell her that I'm married."

"Married. I love the sound of that," he told her as he held her in his arms. "You are mine forever, little lady. Are you ready for that?"

Kat laughed at him. "It is a little too late for you to be asking that, don't you think?"

"Possibly. But at least you can say that I did ask." He released her and took her hand and led her upstairs to their bathroom. "Come on, let's see if I'm right, which I know that I am." He handed her one of the pregnancy tests they had bought before returning to their house.

"Hmmmm, anxious are we?" she teased, taking the box from his hand.

"Very much so," he said.

"You can wait in the other room, you know."

"And I can stay right here with you too. It's not like I haven't seen you naked before." He laughed.

"Eric," she whined with her hands on her hips.

"Alright, alright. I will wait in the bedroom." He left her alone in the bathroom.

Kat was nervous as she read the instructions for the test. After finishing up, she washed her hands and joined Eric in the bedroom.

"Now we wait," she informed him.

"So, Mrs. Lefevre, do you want a boy or a girl?"

"Well, Mr. Lefevre, I would be happy with either. It really doesn't matter to me. What about you?"

"I'm leaning towards a son first, but just as long as the baby is healthy, I'm good." He spoke as if it was already confirmed.

"If I'm pregnant," Kat reminded him.

"No, not if. You are and I know it. I can feel it in my heart and I can see the changes in you." He caressed her cheek. "You have been glowing a lot lately. Your breasts have gotten bigger and you have gain a little bit of weight."

"Oh, so you are saying that I'm getting fat?" she joked.

"Nope, I am saying that you are swelling because of my baby in your tummy." He kissed her lips as he rubbed her stomach. "And I love each and every minute of it."

"You make me so happy, Eric."

"It is the same for me, baby. I can't imagine being without you."
The timer went off and they looked at each other.

"You go check it," Kat insisted. Eric rushed into the bathroom and it seemed like he was in there forever. "Eric, is everything okay?" She called out.

"Yes, it is, Momma." He had a huge smile on his face upon exiting the bathroom.

"I'm pregnant?" she asked.

"We are pregnant," he corrected. He walked over to her and gathered her in his arms. "I can't believe it. I mean, I knew it, but I still can't believe that I'm going to be a dad. Oh, my beautiful Kat, you are making all of my dreams come true. I love you so very much." He held her tight and rocked side to side with her.

"I am going to be a mommy," she sang in his ear.

He held her in his arms as he placed soft kisses on her face and down to her neck. His kisses were powerful and she felt it seeping into her soul and engulfing her. It went from soft and sensual to intimate and demanding. He climbed on top of her and pulled her up to a sitting position so that he could remove her shirt. Then he pushed her back on the bed and took one of her nipples in his mouth.

"Oh, Eric," she moaned. She arched her back, pushing her breasts up to him. He turned his attention to her other breast, bringing a hand up to cup it.

"I love your breasts, Kat. They are perfect for my hands and mouth," he mumbled around her nipple. He continued his sweet assault on her nipple while letting his hand glide down her body. He began to follow the path of his hand with his mouth until he reached the junction between her thighs. "Oh,

Kat, I love the way you smell," he said as he rubbed his nose up and down her opening.

Kat's eyes rolled back in her head and her back arched again. "Baby," was all that she could manage to say.

"Yes, love?" he said as he let his tongue flicker over her bud.

She inhaled sharply. When he leaned in and sucked her clit into his mouth, her hands flew to his head and a growl escaped her lips. "Ahhhhhh,"

He raised his head. "Do you like what I do to you, love?" He did not give her time to answer before he inserted a finger into her canal. He rotated his thumb on her clit while stroking her spot. "Answer me, Kat." He stilled his fingers, waiting on her reply.

"Yes," she finally said.

"Yes what, baby? If you want me to let you cum, then answer my question." His voice was dangerously low.

"Yes, I like what you do to me." She cried out as he began the sweet torture all over again. He raised up to capture her nipple as he continued working her pussy.

Kat's mind was devoid of everything except what he was doing to her body. She felt her orgasm slowly creeping up on her. Eric eased back down between her legs and replaced his thumb with his tongue as he continued pumping his fingers in and out. To still her squirming, his free hand came up and clamped around one leg to hold her in place as he continued to feast.

"Oh, Eric, I'm gonna—" she let out a howl as he rolled his tongue one last time over her sensitive spot. Bright lights flashed behind her closed eyelids and her breath came in pants as if she had just run a marathon. Her legs would not stop trembling and Eric would not stop licking.

"Please," she moaned.

"Please what?" He chuckled.

"Please don't stop, please give it to me, I don't know, just please," she cried out.

"Oh, I love you so much, my beautiful Kat." Eric entered her slowly.

Her arms came up and wrapped around his neck, pulling him closer to her. "Eric," she managed to say.

That night, Eric took his time in making slow, sweet, passionate love to Kat, and she to him. Fully sated much later, they fell into a deep sleep in each other's arms.

CHAPTER 41

ERIC WAS not too thrilled about going back to work. He wished that he could spend more time with his pregnant wife. His family had left him a nice amount of change, but he knew it wouldn't last forever, not with the lifestyle they lived and the number of children he wanted. He knew he had to make that money for his soon-to-be expanding family. He was serious when he told Kat that he wanted a lot of babies, so he had to make sure his ends were in order. He had to drag himself away from her so that he wouldn't be late.

As soon as he entered the building, the first person to cross his path was Angela. He hated the sight of her. He could not look at her without imagining her between Kat's legs, so he always tried to steer clear of her.

"Good morning, Eric. How are you?" she asked him.

"I'm great, thanks for asking. How are you?" He wanted to tell her not to say shit to him, but he kept his cool and thought to himself, Fake bitch.

"I'm doing well. How's Kat?

"Why do you ask?" Immediately, he felt his defenses go up.

Angela knew that he didn't like her asking about his wife, but that didn't stop her.

"No reason. Let's not forget that she was my friend before all of that stuff went down. As I recall, she and I were really close."

"Well, my wife is fine. Thanks for asking."

"What did you say?" She looked stunned.

"You heard what I said. Kat and I are married." He held up his hand so that she could get a good look at his wedding band.

"She married you?" Angela cried. She had a look of disbelief on her face.

"Yes, she did. You seemed surprised by it. You of all people should have known that it was bound to happen soon." He smiled at her before taking the stairs up to his office. Angela was going up in the elevator and he'd had enough of her presence for that day.

He wanted to call Kat, but when he logged in on his computer, he saw that the CEO of the company had requested his presence. He had to put off calling his wife until he was out of the meeting.

He made his way to the plush executive office on the other side of the building. The secretary told him to go ahead and enter. Mr. Blythe was on the phone, but he looked up when Eric walked in the door. He motioned for him to come on in and close the door. Eric sat down in one of the chairs across from his boss and waited. When the old man finished his conversation, he turned his attention to Eric.

"Mr. Lefevre, your team has been on top ever since you have been in charge of them. Your production is always above average and I admire that."

"Thank you, sir." Eric said, wondering this was going. He hoped Angela was not up to something.

"As you know, my brother runs our sister company across town. He is currently in the process of looking for a second-in-command to help him get that location in tip-top shape."

"Yes sir, I saw that the position was available."

"Why did you not apply for it?"

"With all of the things that have been going on lately, I figured that it would not be wise to apply for it. With the marriage, the honeymoon and baby."

"Well, you know that we strongly believe in family. So, that would not have been a problem. We all were happy for you and Katlynn. It is unfortunate that she is no longer working here. We are still in the process of getting to the bottom of that email. Be sure to tell her that she is welcome to come back at any time."

"Thank you, Mr. Blythe, I will tell her that because you want me to, but as her husband, I prefer for her to stay home. We really do appreciate you looking into this situation."

His boss roared with laughter. "I apologize for laughing, but I knew you would say that." He continued to chuckle.

"Excuse me?" Eric was confused.

"I made a bet with my brother that once you guys were married, you probably wouldn't allow her to work."

"Well, I don't know about the allowing part. Katlynn is very headstrong. I did let her know that I prefer her not to, especially with us expecting our first child."

"Well, a double congratulation is in order."

"Thank you very much." Eric could not help beaming at the man.

"This all came just in time. We would like for you to be my brother's second in command at Styles, Inc. If you accept, you would be starting next week. We can discuss your salary in depth, but I will tell you that it will be quite a bit more than what you are making here." Mr. Blythe winked at Eric.

"So, you want me to move to that company? Is this a permanent position?" He could not believe it. He would be getting away from Angela and making a lot more money for his family. Of course he was taking the position. There was no need to think about it. He knew the role he would be playing and he knew the bosses. It would be like a fresh start for him.

"Yes, it is a permanent position. We are always looking to grow, and we both feel that you are the man for that job. I know that you just came back from your honeymoon, but to sweeten the pot, we will give you until Friday morning to give us an answer. You can take the rest of the week off to contemplate the offer and discuss it with your new wife. What do you say to that?"

Hell, he did not need to think about it at all. He wanted this position, had been wanting it.

"Mr. Blythe, with all due respect, I don't need to think about it. I would be more than happy to accept the position."

Mr. Blythe looked stunned for a moment then a smile adorned his weathered face. "Well, alrighty then. I will have Amanda bring you the contract to look over and sign. Just have it to me by Friday and you will start over there bright and early on Monday morning. Oh, and you can clear out your office and still have the rest of the week off to spend some time with your wife." He stood and Eric followed suit.

"Thanks so much for this opportunity, sir." He shook hands with his boss.

"No problem, young man. Thank you for being dedicated to the company and helping us grow. Who knows, if everything goes well, it is very likely that you will advance even more. But that is only if you want it. It is all there, just waiting for someone to lay claim to it." Mr. Blythe walked Eric to the door.

"Thanks again, and I will have that contract to you as soon as possible." Eric headed back to his office. He wanted to pump his fist, but contained himself. He could not wait to tell Kat the news.

As soon as he sat down at his desk, he picked up the phone and called her.

CHAPTER 42

ANGELA WALKED to her office and slammed the door. Kat had married Eric. She couldn't believe it. Kat was supposed to be her woman, but had let him sweet talk her right on out of Angela's bed. She knew that he loved Kat. It was obvious for all to see. But that did not do a thing to ease the hurt she felt. It was final; there was no hope of getting her back. She knew that she had to move on, but she didn't want to. She wanted Kat.

She sat down at her desk and summoned Trixie to her office. When the woman arrived, Angela let loose on her. "Your so-called plan backfired like fuck. She fucking married him," she yelled.

"They are married? You got to be kidding me?" Trixie sat there with a look of disbelief on her face.

"Yes. And the smug bastard had the nerve to flash his damn ring in my face. Ugh, I hate him." Angela held her head in disgust. She didn't know what else to do, what to try next.

"I'll think of something since your harebrained schemes don't work." Trixie stood to leave. "I know how to deal with men. They think with their dicks. It is as simple as that. Let me get him in the right situation and Kat can kiss his ass goodbye.

I'm telling you, I ain't no joke with this tongue. And if your ass wasn't so sprung on Kat, you would let me show you." She looked pointedly at Angela.

"My schemes? That shit was your, oh-so-brilliant idea. I just went along with you. Don't make me have to check your ass. And sweetie, you have too many men running through your ass for me to even imagine touching you. Your pussy is probably dripping with diseases. Don't fuck with me, little girl. This is a grown woman's game and you are my puppet. Do what we agreed to do and leave the rest of that shit out."

Trixie slammed the door on her way out.

With a headache forming, Angela sat holding her head, trying to think of a way to get to Kat without Eric interrupting them. Trixie was turning out to be a liability instead of an asset. She should have known better than to trust that ghetto hoodrat with this mission.

She sat back in her chair as a new thought entered her mind. It was time for her to up the stakes. "Hmmm, maybe I've been going about this the wrong way," she said to the empty room.

Eric was a man, and all men were alike. All that was needed was alcohol and a decent-looking female. She was sure that he would buck under pressure. He wouldn't be able to resist the lady, hence the end of his relationship with Kat. She would have to pull out the big guns and find a real dime piece. It was obvious that he wasn't going to be persuaded by Trixie. Hell, she couldn't blame him, because she couldn't see herself fucking with the young girl either. She would call her cousin Bianca to get the job done. Bianca was a man-eater to the extreme. She would definitely break his ass. Now, all she needed to do was get back in Kat's good graces, so that when the shit hit the fan, she would be there to comfort her.

Angela took a sip of her coffee and focused her attention on the files she had to go through. Calling Kat would have to wait until after lunch. Besides, she had to mentally prepare herself for their conversation. If she made the call now, she knew that she would say something out of character and end up pushing Kat further away from her.

Her employees knew their boss wasn't in a good mood. Everyone seemed to skirt around her when she was out on the floor. She took her anger out on anyone who approached her with a problem and even on some who were just innocent bystanders. She didn't care; she needed an outlet for her anger and they were the scapegoats. After a grueling three hours of bitching at them, she made her way back to her office. It was finally time for her to make her call.

She picked up her phone and dialed Kat's number, praying like hell that Eric had been pulling her leg. She hoped that he was not being completely honest with her. She wouldn't believe it until she heard it from Kat. She crossed her fingers and braced herself.

CHAPTER 43

KAT WAS washing the dishes when she heard her phone ringing. She saw that it was her former job's number and assumed that it was Eric calling. She smiled as she answered the phone. "Hello husband."

"So, it is true. You are married to him." Angela's voice came across the line and she sounded pissed off.

Kat walked over to the table and dropped down into one of the chairs. Her smile disappeared. She'd thought that she was done with Angela after the photo incident. She wanted nothing further to do with the woman.

"Why are you calling me? Are you finally going to admit that it was you who emailed those photos to everyone?" She was tempted to hang up, but something told her to see what Angela had to say.

"He told me that you guys got married, and I just wanted to see if he was telling me the truth. No, I did not do that. I promise you that I didn't. I don't know how whoever sent those pictures got them. I kept them in my house, in my bedroom. Have you ever considered the fact that it could have been geared toward me instead of you? I haven't told anyone else this except my boss, but someone demanded money from me in order to get the pictures back. So you see, it couldn't have been me."

"Is that right? Well, I guess we will all see one day soon, very soon. I'm going to do everything in my power to catch the person responsible for that shit. How could you have been the target when your face wasn't even visible? No one knew it was you, not one single person. But whatever. Yes, it is true. He and I are husband and wife. So, now that you know, have a good day." She was prepared to hang up when she heard Angela calling out to her.

"Kat, wait. Do you really love him? Is he really what you want?" She detected desperation in Angela's voice.

"I love him with everything in me. He is my soul mate, we fit together. I am very happy with him." Angela didn't speak for a moment. "Okay, I just needed to know if there was any hope left for you and I." Her voice was almost a whisper.

"No, there is none. We had a fun time while it lasted, but it is a done deal. I am exactly where I want to be. I have the man of my dreams and we are expecting our first child. Please, just let me be and enjoy my blessing. Can you at least be happy for me?"

"You are having a baby? Wow, I don't know what to say. I guess I should say congratulations and I wish the best for you guys. I am sorry that I disturbed you, but I needed to know and I needed to hear the words from you."

"Thanks a lot for that. Have a nice life, Angela." Kat hung up the phone and sat at the table trying to collect her thoughts. She really did hope Angela was done playing games and was ready to move on with her own life. There would never be any going back for them. Whatever they had shared was in the past and that was where it would stay.

She got up and cleaned the house with renewed energy and decided to go grocery shopping so that she could prepare a special meal for her husband.

While in the store, she heard her phone ring. "Hey babe," she said.

"Hi, baby," Eric replied, "What are you up to my love?"

"I am at the grocery store. Is there anything you want?"

"I want you," he whispered.

"You have me, baby." She giggled. She loved his playful banter.

"True, but I would love to be inside of you right at this moment. I would give anything to feel those thighs wrapped tightly around my waist." His voice was low and dangerous. She knew that he was massaging himself.

"I'm shopping, Eric."

"I know, you told me that already."

"Well stop it, then."

"Okay, baby, but you have some serious making up to do. If you were home, we could have had some fun."

"I wanted to surprise you with a special dinner," she told him.

"Oh really? Can I still have it?"

"Yes," she whispered into the phone. "You can have whatever it is that you like."

"I like you, can I have you?"

"Ummm, you had better love me, and you already have me."

"I have you forever, baby?"

"Yes, you do. I love you, but I have to go. I have been standing in this same spot for too long," she said, remembering that she was in the middle of a very busy supermarket. She glanced up and down the aisle to see if any of the customers were paying attention to her. She saw a lady to her left staring in her direction. When she caught the woman's eyes, the woman turned away and pretended she was studying the items on the shelf. Kat shook head and continued with her conversation, because she was probably imaging something that wasn't.

His rich laughter came across the line. "Okay, Kat, my love, I will see you at home. I love you, baby. Be safe."

"I love you too, Eric, and I will." She hung up the phone and went up front to pay for her items.

When she returned home, she started dinner and went upstairs to soak in preparation for her husband's special night. She wanted everything to be perfect for him.

ERIC was in a rush to get home. He had missed his wife and he was couldn't wait to share his news with her. They would finally be rid of Angela. No more seeing her face at work and being reminded that she once was Kat's lover. He pulled into the driveway and rushed into the house. Silence greeted him at the door. Kat wasn't anywhere downstairs.

Making his way to their bedroom, he heard music coming from the bathroom. He smiled to himself as he visualized her naked body all wet and soapy. Easing his way in the room, his first glimpse of her stole his breath away. Her head was resting on a bath pillow, her eyes closed, the top of her breasts peeking at him through the bubbles. He had control the urge to take her right there in the tub.

"Hey, love."

"Eric, you scared me. What are you doing home so early?" She sat up in the tub.

"I am off until Monday. Finish up with your bath and come downstairs. I have some good news to share with you. I'll be in the kitchen." He took off his jacket and tie then retreated.

Kat hurried with her bath and dressed quickly. She made her way to the kitchen and found Eric sitting at the island drinking a beer.

"Okay, you have my attention. What's the news?"

He smiled and took her hand, pulling her to him. "I got a promotion today."

"Really? That's great. What kind of promotion?"

"I got promoted to a manager's position at Styles today. I will start on Monday. Boss man gave me the rest of the week off to prepare myself for it. Plus, more time to enjoy my new wife."

"Oh my goodness, that's great, honey." She threw her arms around his neck and gave him a hard kiss. "I'm so happy for you."

"So am I, baby. Everything looks great, the pay especially. With the salary I'll be making, you won't have to worry about returning to work anytime soon. You can focus on caring for our baby."

"You just want me barefoot and pregnant all of the time." She giggled.

"That would be true, little darling. I told you before that I want a lot of little mini-mes running around."

"And then, my sweet husband, you won't be able to get it whenever and wherever you want."

"We will wait, then," he said before his tongue slipped into her mouth, ending the conversation.

THE months that followed were pure bliss for Kat and Eric. Kat was amazed by the way her body was changing and she loved the way Eric doted on her. She was even on speaking terms with her mother again. Her relationship with her family was still very strained, but with the baby on the way, they were all attempting to work past their differences. Her sister had even started back asking her to babysit again. Sometimes she gave in, figuring it would give her and Eric some practice before their own baby arrived. He was always delighted to hang out with the kids and was never opposed to her keeping them. She was grateful to him for that. He accepted them as his niece and nephews and they adored him just as much as he them.

Kat finally felt at peace. She had her husband, her knight in shining armor.

CHAPTER 44

TRIXIE WATCHED Eric claim tables clear across the room from her. She felt her heart about to thump out of her chest. She wanted him bad. He would be able to satisfy her body as well as her financial needs. She was pissed that Angela had included her cousin in the mix. She wasn't about to play second fiddle to another woman. She was making her move tonight, right before Bianca made her entrance. Angela might be pissed at her, but oh well. Her game plan was tight in her mind. He would be going home with her while Angela's flunky looked on as they left.

Rent and utilities had eaten up her recent check and money for drinks was a hard thing to come up on, so she scoped the scene looking for a hungry perv to stick with her drinking tab. If she played her cards right, he would supply her for the rest of the night. Looking around, she spotted her mark sitting at the bar glancing her way. She inhaled deeply, gathered her nerves, and beckoned him over. It didn't take much to get his attention. She laughed inwardly as he almost broke his neck trying to get to her before she changed her mind. He was a heavyset man, nearly bald, and looked to be in his fifties. His suit looked as if it had come from her great-grandfather's closet. The buttons on his shirt struggled to remain closed. She could see his undershirt through the gasps. She grimaced at the thought of him touching her.

"What's a pretty lady like you doing sitting all over here by your lonesome?" he asked as soon as he sat down. She got a whiff of his rancid breath and she almost gagged.

"I guess I was secretly awaiting you." She held her breath as he started talking.

"That's what I'm talking about. You a sexy little thang. What you drinking on, suga?" He slid his chair closer to hers. She didn't know how much longer she would be able to tolerate his breath. It smelled like shit. Like he had been eating sick, hot, wet, stinking ass. Her lunch threatened to come up with his next words.

"If you play your cards right, I just might be willing to take care of you tonight." He licked his dry, crusty lips as his gaze raked over her body.

"How about we start with a drink? I want a Sex on the Beach and a shot of Patrón." She figured if she had to suffer through his funk, then she might as well get throwed to help her deal with his ass.

"Shit, you got expensive taste. I hope you will be worth it later on." His implication was obvious. Trixie knew he was planning on having sex with her, but Eric would put an end to all of his nonsense once she worked him over.

"Of course I'm worth it, Daddy. You betta' believe it."

She would do a lot of things for money, but doing him would require serious thinking. She felt his dry-ass fingers on her arm. His touch made her shiver in disgust. She wanted nothing more than to cuss his ass out and slap him across the face. Then she thought about it; she wanted those drinks.

Trixie found herself frowning as he placed their order. The waitress looked over at her and smirked. She knew the deal. She knew what was going down. She knew that Trixie was about to break this poor fool for his bank and send him home without getting inside of her panties. Trixie was sure she had seen the same game every damn weekend.

She let her attention stray over to where Eric sat with his friends. They seemed to be having a dandy ole' time. To her left, closer to the ladies' room, she spotted Bianca sitting by her lonesome. Her gaze was fixed on Eric. She was a predator and he was her prey. Trixie could tell she was ready to pounce on her victim, so she excused herself from Ole' Stank Breath and intercepted Bianca by approaching Eric's table first.

"Oh, wow. Hey, Eric. I haven't seen you here in a while. What have you been up to?" Her back was to Bianca and she could feel the death stare burning a hole in her back.

"How's it going, Trixie?" She knew he only asked to be polite, but she didn't care one bit.

"I'm good. We all miss you at work. How's the new job coming along?" She placed her hand on his shoulder and smiled.

"I love it. I miss you guys too, but I had to do what was best for my family since I'm going to be a dad soon." The pride in his voice was evident.

"OMG, Kat is pregnant? I had no idea. Congrats on your baby and the new job. I just wanted to come and speak, my date is looking pissed right about now." She grinned at Eric. "He is the jealous type, gets all crazy every time I speak to another man."

"Is that right?" Eric seemed no longer interested in their exchange.

She shifted around a little to make sure her boobs jiggled in his face. "Yeah, he can't seem to keep his hands off me."

"Well, good luck with that." Eric turned his attention back to one of his friends, leaving Trixie standing there.

"Okay, see ya," she finally said to no one in particular since none of the men at that table were paying any attention to her. She made her way back to her spot, back to Shit Mouth and her drinks.

"It sure did take you a long time," he said.

"Those are my co-workers over there. The guy I was talking to just informed me that he and his wife are expecting their very first child." She played the overjoyed card to the max. She hadn't gotten a buzz yet, so she needed to play nice with the man.

"Isn't that something? What about you, do you have any babies?"

"Yes, I do. I have three children."

"No shit? Three kids with a body like that? Damn, girl, you got me wondering what you look like under that dress." He let his eyes stray to her nearly-exposed breasts.

"You sure are looking kind of hard."

"I can't help it. I see something I want very badly," Ole' Crusty whispered.

"How about you sit over there until I have a few more drinks, and then we can discuss this further? Right now, I just met you and I can't be letting you feel me up already." She was beginning to wonder if the drinks were really worth it after all when he scooted his chair away from her. She exhaled a sigh of relief.

"Alright, I will play along with you for now." The warning hung in the air.

Trixie twisted in her seat and let her attention float back to Bianca. The beautiful woman was staring at her while talking on a phone. Trixie knew without a shadow of doubt that she was informing Angela about her actions. She didn't care. This was her night, the night that she would claim Eric for her own. Angela just wanted to come between him and his wife, but Trixie had other plans for him. She needed him to be her sugar daddy. She wanted his money and all that he had to offer. Her phone went off, letting her know she had received a text message. She clicked on the icon and saw it was from Angela.

What the fuck are you doing? Stick to the plan or I'm going to kick your ass and then fire you.

Trixie rolled her eyes and took a moment before responding to her boss. "All I did was speak to the man, that's all."

She got another message. Don't speak. All you need to do is take the fucking picture.

Fine, she responded before throwing her phone in her bag. She retrieved the prepaid phone Angela had given her, switched it over to camera mode, and waited for Bianca to make her move.

AFTER an hour of putting up with the man at her table, she was finally able to get the picture she needed. Her instructions were simple, snap the picture, send it to the little wifey along with the name of the club, sit back, and wait for the fireworks to go off.

She was ready for the action. Her buzz was in full force and she had convinced Ole' Stank Breath to chew some fucking gum if he was going to be all up on her. To her amazement, he chuckled and took the gum, saying, "Anything for you, Li'l Mama."

CHAPTER 45

THE CLUB was packed to the gills. This was so not the crowd Kat anticipated. It didn't matter though, she was there to get her man, and God have mercy on any and every ho that stepped to her in the wrong way. Making her way around the club, she spotted him on the dance floor with a woman. Instantly, she saw red. She wanted to go over and pull her ho card, but instead, found an empty table and ordered a Coke. She couldn't believe that he would stoop so low. Here he was, out grinding on the next bitch while she was home carrying his child, the child that he claimed to want so damn bad.

"OMG, girl, what are you doing here?" a voice called from behind where she sat. She turned and saw Christy. She could tell that her friend was lit.

"I can't believe you up in here. I know Eric be having you on lockdown and all."

"I missed you guys. I wanted to see what y'all were up to." She watched Eric from the corner of her eye.

"Girl, you should have called me. It would have been a Girls' Night Out. Shit, girl, it's popping up in here tonight. Too bad you ran off and got married, plus knocked up. We could have really done some damage up in this piece." Christy was slurring and talking loud. Kat was sure that she was on the way to being drunk as hell. She sipped her drink and looked toward the dance floor. She pointed to Eric. "I know that muthafucka isn't over there freaking with some ho."

"I guess he isn't satisfied with what he has at home." Kat's voice was low.

"Maybe it isn't anything," Christy said. "Maybe he is just dancing with her. Just give it a minute and see what happens."

"You know what, I will do that. I'm not going to jump to conclusions. I'll just wait it out and see how it goes." Kat took a drink of her soda and watched her husband.

As of yet, all she could see was that the chick was trying her best to get down and dirty, but Eric was keeping her at an arm's distance. What she thought was grinding earlier was not what she saw now. True, he was dancing, but he wasn't letting his body have any contact with hers. Kat played her hand and remained calm when all she wanted to do was go over and beat the shit out of the bitch.

"Look, girl, he is walking away," Christy pointed out.

Kat saw her husband removing himself from the woman's clutches. Even though he walked off, she wasn't done. Kat saw her follow Eric to his table and then realized the woman was a familiar face. What happened next made her blood boil. The chick climbed into his lap. Kat was about to jump up, run over, and bum rush the chick, but her friend caught her arm and pulled her back to her seat.

"Listen, Ma, I know you want to whoop some ass right about now, but you need to stop and think about your baby.

That is the most important person right now." She held Kat's arm in a tight grip.

Kat lowered herself back into her chair and took a deep breath. "It's so damn hard. She knows that he is my husband but she's still fucking with him." Her voice was dangerously low.

"You know it's all a part of the game. Once he is off limits, the more attractive he becomes to them." Christy took a swig of her drink.

"I don't think it is because she wants to fuck him. I think it is more or less that Angela put her up to it."

"Why would she do some stupid shit like that?"

"It's a long story," she said absent mindedly as she continued watching Eric. He had pushed Bianca away from him after she had climbed on his lap and tried to kiss him. Kat wanted so bad to hurt her, but she had her child's health to think about.

"How did you know something was up anyways?"

"I got a picture text from some unknown person that said Eric was making a new friend at this club. The picture showed Bianca with her body all up on his and his hands on her hips." Kat was seething mad. She didn't know how much more of this she could take. Ten minutes had passed and Bianca was still at the table. Kat stood up made her way to the table and stood directly in front of Bianca. Every person at the table shut up on her arrival. There was a look of disbelief on Eric's face.

"If you touch my husband one more fucking time, I'm going to break your fucking neck, understand?" She stood over Bianca as if daring her to move an inch.

"Are you trying to threaten me?" Bianca's voice quivered.

Kat leaned in closer to her and whispered, "No, sweetie, it is a promise. Now, leave this table or I will make good on my word." Bianca got up from the seat and walked off without looking back. Kat turned to Eric. "I'll see you at home." Then she turned and left the club.

She was beyond pissed at him. Even though nothing happened and she saw him pushing the woman away, she felt like he shouldn't have let things get that far. She expected him to finish his night out and return home late, but to her surprise, he got home not long after she did. He entered the bedroom slowly, as if afraid of what lay ahead of him. She watched him undress and climb in bed beside her.

"I'm disappointed in you," she finally said.

"Nothing happened," he began.

"She was all over you," Kat cried, turning toward him.

"True, she was, but each and every time, I removed her. I was being polite about the situation. She just kept coming at me, so, finally, I started feeding her drinks getting her to loosen up. I'm not dumb, Kat. Mark told me that she was Angela's cousin and I figured something wasn't right with the whole setup." Kat didn't say anything. "While we were dancing, she let it slip that Angela had gotten Trixie to send those pictures to everyone. She also told me that Angela is in love with you and will do anything in her power to break us up. Then she went on to tell me that once you see the picture of us dancing, you would leave me and that would be okay because she would comfort me. When I asked her what picture, she told me that Trixie was supposed to take one and send it to you. That's when the dance ended.

"I left her on the floor, but she followed me and tried to kiss me, saying she was sorry and all. When you came up, she was begging me not to let Angela know she had told me all of that."

He closed his eyes and took a deep breath. "I love you and only you, Kat. I would never jeopardize what we have for a fling. You are all I want, all I need. I've waited for you too long to mess up what we have, baby. This right here between us is my life. You are mine forever and that is it."

"Wow, that is a lot to process." Kat was shocked by all that he had said. But it all made sense. All the pieces finally fit in the puzzle. Angela had been behind everything because she was jealous.

"How did you know to come there?" Eric asked.

"I got a picture message."

"I'm going to handle this once and for all. Baby, trust me not to hurt you. We are in this together for life."

"I trust you. I just … I don't know. I saw her arms around you and I panicked. I don't want to lose what we have ever. I love you too much to ever let you go." She put her head on his shoulder and he held her close.

"Angela will get hers eventually, as will Trixie. All I need for you to do is concentrate on us and our baby. The rest of it is irrelevant. Our love will overcome any adversities that they try to throw our way. We are one and we will always be." His lips met hers.

ABOUT THE AUTHOR

Shemeka grew up in a small town in Arkansas and has always had a passion for reading and writing. After being diagnosed with Lupus, and unable to work, she decided that it was time to work on her novels. She wrote her very first novel in 2013 and after being encouraged by a dear friend, she pursued her dreams by learning the necessary tools to start her writing journey.Proud to be a published author, Shemeka is also an advocate for Lupus awareness. Currently, Shemeka resides in southwest Missouri with her two children; D'Andre and Blossom.

Thank you for reading Vindictive and I hope you enjoyed this story about undying love. When it's real, it feels good.

Please take time to post your review and turn the page and get a sneak peek of Anna Black's *I Just Wanna Be Loved.*

Enjoy!

Just Wanna Be Loved

By

Anna Black

CHAPTER ONE

I stood and gave my dining room table another once over, making sure everything was in place. My son was coming home after being in Iraq for eighteen months and I was eager to see him. He was here for a visit a few months ago, when he came home on leave, but to me it felt like ages ago, and I couldn't wait to see him.

"Do you need anything else? I have to run home to shower and change before my favorite nephew gets here," my sister and best friend, Catherine, asked.

"No, no, no, I have it from here. I am going to head to the airport soon. Mo' is coming over to greet the guest and hold down the fort until I return."

"Are you sure, because I don't want to get down the street and have to turn around. And don't think I'm running into nobody's store in this heat to pick up anything, Miss Char."

"I have everything I need, Catherine, and if I don't, I will find somebody to get it for me. You've done enough, darling, and I thank you. Trey always said you're the only one on this planet who can cook better than me, and he is going to be so happy to see that his favorite auntie cooked all of his favorites."

"Well, Trey is the only son we both have, and I know we have spoiled him rotten. He turned out better than my baby girl, Mesha. She is a piece of work."

"I know that's right, but we still have to love our kids and have their backs no matter what, Cat."

"I know, I know." Catherine sighed.

"Go ahead and get out of here and go get dressed. I'm going to head to the airport."

Just as I said that, Mona walked in smiling brightly. "Divas... Hey!" she yelled.

"Hey, Mo'. You are right on time. I was just about to call you," I said.

"Well, you know me, baby. I'm always on time," she said and kissed and hugged us both.

Catherine sucked her teeth. "Hump, except for church. I get tired of holding your seat with my purse."

We laughed.

"Well, church starts too damn early. Hell, my husband died and left me a ton of money that allowed me to retire at forty-two, and I don't get up before ten," Mona proclaimed.

I had to go. "Well, I have to get to O'Hare and Catherine needs to run home and change. All the side dishes and desserts are done, and Bernie is handling all of the meat. All I need you to do is make your fabulous punch and greet anyone who arrives before we get back. And please, don't let Bernie open up one bottle of liquor. He should be here any minute to get started on the meat."

"Girl, go ahead. I got this. Bernard ain't no match for me. I will make my famous punch and make sure he gets started. Where is the meat, so I can show him when he gets here?"

"In the kitchen. There are four coolers near the French doors. Everything is seasoned and iced, so he can roll them out back. One has chicken, one has steaks, one has burgers and hot dogs, and that red one has kabobs. My dear sister, Catherine, turned me on to Ziploc bags, so it will be easier than coming in and out of the house. And there is a stack of aluminum pans on the island and like five gallons of sauce. Bernard travels with his own utensils, grills, and pine wood, so he knows what to do."

"Got you, love. Now tell me there is chilled wine, because y'all know Miss Mo' can't work sober."

We all laughed again.

"Girl, you know it. The wine fridge is full, so help yourself. We have to go," I said. Catherine and I both hurried out.

Before I could pull out of my circular drive, I noticed my brother, Bernard, was unloading his truck. He had brought two more grills with him. I smiled. Bernard had the best barbeque on the planet and never declined an opportunity to show off his skills.

"Hey, Bernie, I'm headed to the airport to get Trey. All the meat is ready for you!" I yelled.

"A'ight, lil' sis. I'm on it. Drive safe!"

"Mo' is inside. Gon' in!"

I drove off, anxious to see my baby. Trey was my heart. My grown-ass little man. I couldn't wait to see him.

He and I grew up together, to be honest. I was fifteen when I had him. By the time I was seventeen, I was enrolled in college, working two jobs, and living with my evil-ass mother. She kept him a lot for me back then, and by the time I got my associates degree, we moved out. I was able to afford a little townhouse because I managed to get a job working as a junior accountant. By the time I got my masters, things moved quickly, and after busting my ass, I was in charge of marketing.

By the time Trey was in the seventh grade, I purchased my thirty-five hundred square feet home that had an in-ground pool. Things were good.

Yes, I dated, of course I did. But I never had, or should I say found, the man who was quite right for me. I had brief engagements twice. Once to a man who I later found out was already married, and then to another who decided he like to put his hands on women. There was always a reason things just didn't work out, and now at forty, I was single, still dating, but definitely single.

I parked and hurried to get inside. Trey's flight had already landed and I wanted to be there at baggage claim when he made it. I walked over and read the digital boards and when I found the one with the correct flight number, I stood and waited. I kept looking around for him, but I didn't see him. As soon as I pulled out my phone again to call him, someone covered my eyes from behind.

"Guess who?"

I spun around and he lifted me up from the floor with a big hug. "Hey, son, how are you?"

"I'm good, Ma."

He continued to hold me tight, and even though I said I wouldn't cry, I couldn't hold back my tears. He put me down and I wiped my eyes.

"Ma, you promised."

I wiped more tears. "I know, son, but it is just so good to see you. Look at you, handsome." He had on his uniform and I thought he looked more and more like his absent father each time I saw him.

"Ma, stop it."

"You are," I said. We hugged again.

"Where is Auntie Cat— I mean Catherine? I thought she'd come too." My sister had gone by Cat her entire life, but after she became a judge, she told everyone to stop calling her that. I didn't care. She was my sister, so I still called her Cat.

"She had to go change. She and I were up all night fixing your favorites, and this morning we were up early to make desserts. She'll be at the house when we get back. And call her Auntie Cat, Trey."

"And catch a beat down? No, thank you. If she wants to be Auntie Catherine, she will be Auntie Catherine. Momma, you know she don't play."

"I know, but not like you, I ain't scared of her."

"Well, I am." We laughed. "Man, I can't wait to eat. That flight was long and all I could think about was your potato salad and Auntie Catherine's baked beans. And if Uncle Bernie ain't grilling, I ain't eating no meat," he joked.

"Well, you know your uncle got the grill, and Catherine put her foot in those baked beans. I tasted them this morning. A little spicier than usual, but still delicious."

"Well, I'm ready." The conveyer belt started to rotate. "Let me check for my bags, Ma. Hold this," he said and handed me what looked like a computer bag.

"I'm going to run and get the car, so meet me outside, son."

I hurried to the parking lot. By the time I made it around, he hadn't come out yet. I sat tapping the steering wheel to the beat of the song on the radio, hoping the officer would give me a break. But of course, he waved for me to move. I drove around once, praying I wouldn't have to circle again and was relieved to see Trey standing under the American Airlines sign. I pulled up to him and popped the trunk. After he loaded his things, he got in.

I reached over and rubbed his head. "Oh, son, it is so good to have you home safe and sound. You know, you being deployed turned your momma into a prayer warrior. If I didn't know God before, I found him when you boarded that plane to go over to that place."

"I know what you mean, Ma. I mean, I knew what I was signing up for when I joined, but I'm so glad to be back I don't know what to do."

"I heard that. Now will you please find a wife and give me some grandbabies? Hell, I'm single and lonely. My only son left me, so I'd like a grandbaby to spoil."

"Momma, I just got home. Let me at least shower first."

We laughed.

"Okay, but after your shower, get a wife and make me some grandkids."

"How about you date again? You are only forty and you're still fine, Momma. Every time I show someone your picture, they don't believe you're my mother."

"Well, son, your mother has tried dating. I've met some nice guys, but I don't know, son. It's like that spice, that wow factor, is missing. Most men I date have baggage and problems and alimony and kids in college and so on. I don't know, son. When that right one comes along, who sweeps me off my feet and makes me happy, I'll make it work. Until then, I work on making myself happy."

"He's out there, Ma, I know he is. You're too beautiful and smart. He'll come soon."

"I hope so, baby, but in the meantime, give me some grandbabies to spoil."

"I will, Ma, maybe sooner than you think."

I was shocked by his comment. "Tracy Keyshaun Jones, what are you trying to say?"

"I don't know yet, Ma, but La-La and I have gotten closer while I was away. I mean, she helped me get through some tough times over there, Ma, and I think she's the one."

"Lavitra from high school? I didn't know you and her were talking again, Trey. When did this happen?"

"Well, when I went back after my break. I checked my Facebook and she sent me a friend request. Now you know I was shocked, right, after how bad our break-up was."

I interrupted. "Yes. I don't know how that girl thought you'd give up your dreams of going into the military to stay here with her. Hell, I didn't want you to go into the military either, but it's your life."

"That wasn't exactly the reason, Ma. The problem was I didn't want to get married or at least engaged to her before I left. I was eighteen and I wasn't ready to make that kinda decision back then.

"So we started conversing by email and I told her she just missed me, that I had just left Chicago, and from there, we started emailing every day. And then I called her and we started talking on the phone, video chatting, and we just reconnected."

"So did you tell her you're only going to be in Chicago for two weeks before heading to Fort Hood?"

"Yeah, I told her and she isn't too happy about it, so I've decided to take her with me."

My heart stopped and I shot him a look. "Boy, what the hell? You know I'm not with that living together mess. And you have to find a place before taking on the responsibility of taking care of a woman."

"Momma, calm down. I didn't mean taking her with me in two weeks. I'm talking about asking her to marry me and then get the house and all. Marry her and then take her to Texas."

I let out a deep breath. "Well why you didn't say that? I almost crashed my Jag." I slapped his arm.

"Ma, you taught me better. You know I'm not the type to leap first. La-La has always been in my heart since high school and I've never been able to completely get over her, no matter how I've tried. Hopefully, these two weeks at home will be good, and if so, I'll pop the question before I leave."

I shook my head and smiled. "I knew my baby would grow up, but damn it's hard to swallow another woman being in your life. I know you and La-La have been in love for years, and that love you can't shake is the love that is meant, so I wish you two the best. I'm just scared that once you are married, I won't be number one anymore."

"Awww, Ma, you will always be my number one, just don't tell La-La."

"Okay, okay, son. I can live with that. You know I'll always have your back, baby, no matter what you decide. Plus, you need someone to care for you. Just let her know that she has to hang with me and your Auntie Cat to learn how to cook your favorites," I teased.

"I will, Ma, you know this."

We laughed. We continued endless conversation and when we got back to the house, there were five cars out front. Three I recognized and the other two I had no idea. "I wonder who those two cars belong to." I undid my seatbelt to get out.

He undid his. "I don't know, Ma. La-La is coming, I think that Infinity is hers."

"Well, let's get inside and find out."

We went inside and sure enough, La-La ran into Trey's arms. They held each other tight and I saw my son share a tongue kiss with a woman for the first time. I turned my head because it was apparent they missed each other, and then I noticed a young, handsome face.

He interrupted Trey and La-La's reunion. "A'ight, La-La, let me get a hug in too."

He looked vaguely familiar, but I couldn't place him. I had a very strong feeling I knew him, but I couldn't put my finger on from where. All I knew was he was fine as hell, young, but delicious.

"Hey, man, what's going on? It's been like forever. Man, you have changed," Trey said. He could barely hug this stranger because La-La wouldn't let him go.

"Welcome home, man. We have to definitely do better with keeping in touch. It's been far too long."

"I know. I mean, you went to college, I joined the army, and I did my best, man. I holla'd atcha when I could."

"I know ,Trey, man, same here. I ain't mad atcha. You're back now, and we gon' do it big."

"Hey, don't think y'all gon' kick it without me. Wrong answer!" La-La snapped.

"Hold on, hold on. Save the bickering. Come here, Lavitra, and give me a hug," I interrupted.

She released my son and gave me a tight hug. "Hey, Miss J. It's so good to see you." She smiled when she released her embrace.

"You too. You are just as pretty as you were back in high school."

"She sure is," Trey said and pulled her back into his arms.

I looked at the young man again. "I'm sorry, have we met? Do I know you?"

Trey tilted his head. "Ma, you don't know who this is?" he asked in disbelief.

Puzzled, I looked again, trying to figure out who this young, fine, sexy god was. "No, I can't remember. I mean there is familiarity, but I can't say. I'm afraid I'll say the wrong name."

"Miss J, you don't remember me?"

I did, but I didn't. Trey hung with a few guys because he played sports. However, the only face I'd never forget is his best friend Lil' Ricky. He was my baby, sort of like my young best friend. He hung around me more than he hung with Trey, and helped me way more than my son. Anything I'd asked that kid, he'd do, but I hadn't seen his little pimply face since he left to go off to college. I was surprised he never called or visited after he left. He was my best young buddy. I'd ask Trey had he heard from him and he'd say yes when he did.

I swallowed hard and tried not to look like a horny-ass old lady, because whoever this was, his woman was a lucky girl. "Come on, somebody tell me who this tall, handsome guy is."

Still trying to jolt my memory, "Two houses down," Trey said.

"No fucking way. Oh my goodness, Lil' Ricky? Get the hell out of here," I said and leaped into his arms. He had grown into a fine specimen. He looked like a completely different person.

"Yes, ma'am, it's me," Lil' Ricky said.

"Oh my goodness, you look so ... so ... different. I mean, I can't believe I didn't recognize you. Even your voice. You sound like a grown-ass man."

"I am a grown-ass man, Miss J," he returned.

I laughed. "Yes, you are. Where have you been? I mean, even when your father died, I don't remember seeing you at the funeral."

"I know, Miss J, I was overseas, and by the time I got the news, I couldn't get home in time. I moved back a couple years ago, and now that my stepmom is ill, she moved in with her daughter, so I'm going to do some upgrades and cleaning up the house so I can sell it."

"Oh my, this is, like, crazy. To see you and Miss La-La over here is great. You guys were like the Three Musketeers. When you graduated and went off to college, I never heard from you again. You know you were wrong for that, young man."

"Well, I didn't lose touch with Trey. We talked when we could, and every time I talked to him, I said to tell you I said hello."

"Well, he didn't tell me, and it's good to see you." I remember I had people coming so I had to cut our reunion short. "I need to get in this kitchen and make sure things are in order."

Trey picked up his duffle bag. "And I need to shower."

"Well, I can help you in the kitchen," La-La offered.

"Yes, baby, come on, and Lil' Ricky, you can go out with Uncle Bernie. I'm sure he needs help and I know he has a cold beer for you." I smiled.

La-La and I headed to the kitchen, Trey headed upstairs, and Ricky walked through the kitchen and went out the French doors.

Catherine hadn't made it back yet and Mona was bringing in a covered pan of meat.

"Char, you're back. Where is Trey?"

"He went up to shower. You remember La-La?"

"Child, of course I do. She and Lil' Ricky were the first ones here."

"So Pat and Gene and Mesha must be out back. I saw their cars."

"Yeah, they're out back. Why didn't you tell me Mesha was pregnant? When I saw her belly, my mouth dropped to the floor. Ain't she seventeen?"

I washed my hands. "Yes, girl, and she just turned seventeen a month ago. I told her how hard it was for me when I had Trey at fifteen too, too many times, but that didn't stop her from getting knocked up by that damn Sammy. His ass done left and went on to school on his football scholarship and she is still here looking crazy. Catherine fusses about it every single damn day."

"Well, she is going to have to learn the hard way, like we all did."

I laughed. "You sho' right."

Catherine walked in. "Hey, y'all. I saw your car, Char, where is my baby?"

I pulled out my fancy deviled egg dish to put some of the eggs on it. "He went to shower."

She put a bag on the counter. "Is that you, La-La?"

"Yes, ma'am."

"Girl, get over here and give me a hug. How you been?" Catherine asked and squeezed her tight.

"I'm fine, Miss Catherine. How are you?"

"I'm good, child. Look at you, just pretty as you want to be."

I spoke up because I wanted to brace Catherine for Lil' Ricky. "Here, La-La, take this out to Uncle Bernie for me." She grabbed the bowl of seasoned corn I handed her. "Tell him to put those on the grill for me." As soon as she was on the other side, I pulled Catherine's arm and told Mo' to come closer. "Girl, just wait until you see Lil' Ricky."

"Oh, yes," Mo' co-signed.

"What, girl?" Catherine asked wanting to know the juice.

I said. "He is fine as hell. Girl, when I saw him, my pussy clenched. When Trey told me who he was, I almost died."

"Me too. I didn't even recognize him at all," Mo' added. "All I knew is this chocolate, tall piece of art walked in with La-La. When she told me who he was, I was like 'no fucking way.' He has been drinking milk or fine juice."

Catherine got excited. "Where is he? I want to see him."

"Out back," I said.

She headed for the French doors. "Let me go see him."

She went out and Mo' and I continued to chat. "Girl, you better hold me back, because I'm a widow with money, and I ain't afraid to spend it. I can travel and be his sugar momma," Mo' said.

I burst into laughter.

"Girl, stop it, that boy is Trey's age."

"So, I'm not trying to get with Trey. That would be wrong, but Lil' Ricky can come tuck me in tonight."

Catherine walked back in. "Girl, pour a bucket of ice water on me. Hot damn! That boy is fine."

We laughed.

"I told you. I could not believe my eyes. And for a split moment, I wished I wasn't this old."

"And Trey's mother," Mo' added.

"That too."

We continued to laugh and joke. More guests arrived and, finally, Trey came down.

"Auntie Catherine!" he yelled.

"Trey!" She rushed over and hugged him tight. "Look at you, boy. You are looking so handsome, nephew, just like your daddy."

I threw the oven mit at her. "Hey, watch it, Cat." We never talked about Trey's father. I hadn't seen him since Trey was three, so she knew better.

"Thank you, Auntie, and Momma told me you were on this crazy diet. I see you stuck to it. You look gorgeous, Auntie," he teased as Catherine posed.

"I do, don't I?" She smiled.

"Yes, you do."

Mona cut in. "Well, I know I'm not your favorite auntie, but I missed you too, baby."

"Hey, Auntie Mo'," he said and lifted her little petite body from the floor when he hugged her. Mona was the smallest of the three of us. Not even five feet and maybe a size three on a good day.

"Hey, nephew. It's so good to have you home," she said.

The party got underway and I enjoyed my family and close friends. It was after three in the morning when my house was almost clear, and I didn't argue when my son said he was going to La-La's for the night. I knew he was grown and had grown folk needs. Lil' Ricky assured him he'd help me and Catherine finish up. That was Lil' Ricky, always there to help me.

I walked Catherine to her car, while he put the last of the trash on the curb for me.

"Okay now, you call me when you make it, Catherine. You know you can stay another night."

"Char, I want to get home and sleep in my own bed. I don't want to have to get up for hours, so that needs to be done at home in my own bed."

"Okay. I'll call you tomorrow. We will probably eat leftovers and play some cards. I'm sure Trey and La-La will be back tomorrow to eat since we still have so much food."

"Okay, I'll come back tomorrow and I'll tell Mesha." She put her seatbelt on. "Goodnight, Lil' Ricky!" she yelled. He yelled goodnight back to her and I shut her door and watched her leave my drive.

"Are you leaving?" I asked Lil' Ricky.

"Yeah. I need to run in to get my plate," he replied.

We headed back in. In the kitchen, he reached for the foiled-covered plate.

"Did you get dessert?" I offered.

"No, ma'am. I was supposed to remind Miss Catherine."

I grabbed a knife. "Well, I can't let you leave without a slice of my lemon pound cake."

He sat down at the island. "I thought it was all gone."

"Yes, the two I put out are gone, but I always hide one for Trey." I went into my walk-in pantry, got the plastic cake container, and set it on the island. I opened it and cut him two slices and put them on a plate and then covered it with foil. "There you go," I said and slid it his way.

"Thank you." He smiled and gave me a look.

"You're welcome," I said, placing the lid back on. I felt a little vibe in the air.

He sat there and watched me. I rinsed the knife and added it to the dishwasher and turned back to him still watching me.

"You okay," I asked. It wasn't an uncomfortable stare down. It was more like a checking-me-out stare down.

"Yeah, yeah, I'm good. I guess it's time for me to head home." He stood.

I moved around the counter to head to the living room. "Yeah, it's pretty late. Let me walk you to the door."

He followed close behind me and I could feel his eyes on me. I welcomed it because he was young and I hadn't had much male attention lately. I opened the door and he paused.

"Thanks for having me, Miss J. I mean, it was so good seeing you again. I mean, you still look amazing, and Trey coming home is just great."

Paying attention to the fact that he said I still looked amazing and observing the way he was looking at me, I smiled. He was looking at me in the way a man would look at a woman he was interested in and I liked it. I knew him when he was a funny-looking kid, but he had grown into a man I'd be interested in. "Yes, it's good to have him home."

He flashed his beautiful smile again and I could see the braces he'd worn when he was younger had done him justice, because his teeth were perfect. "Yes it is. I'm going to go now." He turned to leave and something in me wanted to ask him to stay, but I knew that would be inappropriate. He was my son's best friend, and entertaining him like a man my age would be insane.

Being extremely attracted to this young man, I invited him to come back. "We are getting together tomorrow. We have a ton of leftovers. You should come."

"Okay, I'll be here. Do you need me to bring anything?"

"No, we have liquor, beer, food, you name it."

"What time is good?"

"I'd say six, maybe seven. I'm sure everybody wants to recoup from tonight," I said nervously. What was I doing? I wasn't supposed to be attracted to him. This was Lil' Ricky, the pimply-faced kid from two houses over.

"Okay, I'll be here." He smiled and turned to leave. He walked down the drive and passed the BMW that I thought was his that was parked a few feet away from my driveway.

"Isn't that your car?" I shouted.

"Yes, but I'm staying at my dad's house."

"Okay," I said and watched him proceed on his short trip home. I went back inside and let out a deep breath, happy everyone had chipped in and helped me clean. I turned out the lights and headed upstairs.

I asked myself why I was having sexual thoughts about Lil' Ricky. He and my son were best friends, why did I want to fuck him? The entire evening, we had exchanged glances. He had helped me in the kitchen and made it a point to check on me throughout the evening. When we danced in the backyard, my hands were the first hands he reached for to step. He was young, sexy, and oh my. "Stop it, Charlotte," I told myself. "You are too old and you can't go there. Trey would lose it!"

I tried to tell myself that I wasn't feeling him, but it was obvious that I wanted to do things to Lil' Ricky that someone closer to his age should be doing. "Oh my, Char, what has gotten into you? It is not right or natural," I said and got into bed.

I closed my eyes and he was back in my thoughts, so I decided to just go ahead and dream about him. Hell, no one had to know about my dreams.